TRANSFERENCE

[LOVE + HATE IN RAIN CITY]

JOHN BOWIE

RED DOG

UK

Second Edition
First Edition published by Bristol Noir 2020

Paperback ISBN 978-1-913331-83-2
Ebook ISBN 978-1-913331-84-9

www.reddogpress.co.uk

For Chinaski

[trans·fer·ence]
trans·fer·ed, trans·fer·ing

1. The shift of emotions from one person to another
2. A shift in force or energy from one object to another
3. Relocation of a person or thing to another state or place

Some might say: it began as a mistake.'
— Oasis and Charles Bukowski

'And here I am again, lapping at the beast's teats like a true fool, laying my head in the lion's mouth as I hit it on the arse with a big stick.'
— Untethered

'We were all puppets of someone in a self-perpetuating circle of pollutants, violence and hedonistic escapism.'
— Untethered

Introduction

For most, mid-to-late 90s Manchester was dominated by the IRA bomb and then the recovery, rebuilding and media coverage that followed. However, the rain still battered down on us all and the bands played on. They added to an already prolific catalogue of the best epoch-defining music from the great Rain City. The canal and rivers kept flowing. The games kept playing. And, it didn't put people off their stride. They didn't 'Look Back in Anger', all of them stoics, they worked just as hard as they had always done. They would, and always will be, 'Made of Stone'.

JOHN BOWIE

Prologue

THE BLACK HORSE pub lay on an invisible border between Salford and Manchester. Once almost a regal palace, it was now left with tired fixtures, fittings and punters. It was dead on its feet. Peeling wallpaper exposed the layers of generation upon generation of thick nicotine tar and smoke.

The locals hadn't moved much or changed in over fifty years; stuck to the beer and piss-soaked carpet. The rest were mainly students. They joined a transient mass of heavy drinkers propping up the bar, and the holes in its profits. The students' grants kept it afloat each term-time. Because of this, the locals didn't destroy them. After all, without them, their precious boozer would have gone long ago to make way for a car park or supermarket.

And so, the locals and students kept their healthy virtual distance. Eyes and bodies rarely made contact. They fought amongst each other, sure, but stayed to their own. The locals fought for real—the students didn't know how to. Not beyond a slap, shove and an occasional pulled punch. Although, one time a lad got a nasty scar from a glass to the face. It didn't break or he'd be blind.

It didn't pay to play rough in there; unless you were going to go all the way.

Late 90s Salford and Manchester were a bit like that. A symbiotic melting pot of respect, lack thereof and fear keeping everyone in check. The weather did the rest. The media called it

Gunchester. And the club tourists: Madchester. It was simply known as Rain City by those who lived there and knew it best.

The landlord would sometimes say they were closing for good. That they'd had their licence pulled. This happened at the end of every other weekend's lock-in. At this signal, everyone ransacked the place. The overlapping ongoing insurance claims would tie it over another month or so, whilst they still kept coming in. Whilst they still paid up. Otherwise, it was propped up by what was left in the barrels and cellar.

One time these two lads burst in, only part covering their faces and shotguns half-cocked. Not exactly pros. They accidentally bashed an old boy who was sitting behind the door. Other than that, no one got hurt. It was all just piss and wind to rob the register. No one blinked. Hardly bothering to look up over their glasses. Business as usual and nothing out of the ordinary. An hour later they were back; spending the money they'd taken on Stella—such is the circle of life. They bought the old boy a drink and a chaser, pickled egg too. And so karma was restored. That same afternoon, I was sitting there with the rest. I'd grown into the place and it had into me. It had been a while. I was neither a student or local, I kept my own distance; made my own space. The aloof can sometimes gravitate to each other. By carving out a bolt hole and boundaries they can start to overlap and blur with others doing the same. There's only so many dark corners to hide in, or bars to prop up. I didn't notice his shadow next to me at first. And it could have passed for my own reflection in the mirror behind the bar—seeing double was nothing new. The air about him was the same as mine: tainted.

I wasn't asking for a conversation. He made his judgment. He'd thought I was a like-minded soul to pour his out to. I reckoned I'd done more time than him; in service…on the streets… I just wanted a break from it all and to finish my drink—

to remain anonymous.

Normally, you can hide out in a place like that for days; alone, apart and away from the common flow of life. Ironically it's someone doing the same that makes a b-line for you. As it was in this instance. Bad pennies that have fallen to the same patch of ground, sticking together by the same shared dirt.

'I used to hate the taste of whiskey until I was shot—ironic I know. Then, each amber shot became a cushion rather than a blow,' he said.

I said nothing.

'Services? I can tell you are. There was only you and me that didn't jump when those two crashed in waving those pieces about… Were you here when the bomb went off? Irish still having a pop at us,' he mumbled, 'two hundred injured—no one was killed. Some bomb maker that was. The Irish, forget how many of them are over here sometimes… fuck load in Liverpool too. Maybe that's why it was only the two hundred hurt. They weren't serious. I was fuckin' serious when I was having a go at them, back in the day. I'd have killed more than two hundred. No injuries if I was having a fucking go. Pop. Pop. Pop. Watch 'em fall.'

I said nothing.

'It's a sorry state we're in. At each other all the time—the enemy's within, the true demons are in each of us. Gun, trigger and finger—we're all part of the same,' he dribbled on. 'You ever kill a man?' he asked as if the answer he knew I'd give would somehow align us. As if we were walking the same sorry path. I wasn't going to give him the satisfaction. Besides I didn't have the answer he wanted. I was dishonoured for not killing when I had those he referred to in my sights. I was burnt literally. I've scars to show for it. And then again by the establishment—who kicked me out of my unit.

I broke his nose.

He fell, bleeding a trail along and off the end of the bar—out cold. As I left, I wondered again why I'd done it, and not restrained my impulse. Maybe he'd said some of what I was thinking about myself... Or maybe I'd deserved a hit alright and I'd given it to him instead. A wake-up call.

Like me, the ex-services barfly had it coming.

I stood up to walk. The stool wobbled then settled making the only sound in the place. The pub had sat on a knife-edge during our exchange. The atmosphere shift was unmistakable. The barman nodded as the students cowered in the corners. At the table by the door, the old boy put a pickled egg in an open packet of ready salted and crushed it all down; breaking the silence. I thought about going to The Crescent pub next door but didn't fancy it that badly.

'I Am The Resurrection' played in the background—it fitted. The guy I'd dropped was falling all the way past gutter level. I was moving on.

1
Ten Storey Love Song

A FALLEN BOY:

Will B. Rowes, Billy to family and friends, was a shy boy. And, as The Smiths had said: it can stop you doing all the things in life you'd like to. He was seen as uncool back in school.

He'd left this past behind when he graduated and went to College. With a newly shaved head and a mistaken arrogance in his standoffishness, he soon became something else.

The cocoon around him had cracked open in Salford and out came a silken black butterfly. The demons Billy had been suppressing at school and home were celebrated out there in the big city. His walk, the look in his eyes, the way he dressed and his purpose all changed. He became unrecognisable by family. When his friends back home saw him again, they just thought he'd finally got laid. He had, but there was much more to it; there was his realisation that they were all the odd ones out, and not him.

His new halls of residence were a breeding ground for developing this new thinking and his future made self.

His first girlfriend hit him when she got turned on and even harder when turned off. Once, she pinned him against the wall as they waited for an elevator. She yelled in his face, hitting him, split his lip—like he'd done something wrong. They boarded and she went down on him. He came between floors and she bit down on him hard again before the doors reopened. A trickle of blood was running down his leg as they alighted.

The second girl played around, a lot. He wasn't sure her focus was all there, or at least not totally focussed on only him—it wasn't to last.

Another one, wouldn't go all the way. With pictures of Labour politicians everywhere and the Manic Street Preachers on repeat—she didn't last either. He'd developed a taste for it before her. So, she wasn't a keeper. He wanted it all by then—the full meal.

Casual encounters in the clubs like The Hacienda, 42nd street, 5th Ave' and the bars got him by. It was initial early steps into some off-piste kind of manhood. Frottaging at the front of gigs, skulking around in the shadows of clubs all became commonplace; research into how the others had developed, whilst he had been held back. Now the anchor was cut and a resentment built towards home. There was no useful connection there anymore.

He first realised the change in himself when two shell-suit wearing chavs tried it on. They wanted a fag and he wanted to get past, to class. Mikey, the lad he was walking with, gave them two tabs each.

Billy gave up nothing; just stared them down.

A threat of a Stanley knife wasn't enough from them. Back then he'd done that to himself, more, gone further for his own release—long before they'd crossed his path.

The one girl that lasted, there until the end...she was on a similar frequency; in harmony with his shifts, ebbs and flows of emotion. He saw her inner beauty. His hurt was mirrored back at him pooling in her black eyes. And she felt it too; saw the same in him.

A sexual aesthetic arose in both their mutual pains. They both admired and fed on it. It belonged only to them, it was their own sort of love.

They started easy; reading Ballard's 'Crash'. Then, 'American Psycho'. Shortly after they read Roland Barthes' 'Mythologies'. 'Labyrinths' by Borges followed and then they started dipping into the artworks of Giger and the architecture by Lebbeus Woods. And with this… came eventual true deconstruction… of the self.

By the time there was a group of them reading 'Cities of the Red Night' by William S. Burroughs—it was a communal thing in the block of flats and their paths had become fixed in a definite direction: a thirst for pleasure, pain and all that's in between.

'Something you'd like to try?' she'd ask on occasion, 'Say so.'

He said no… at first… to begin with… Together, they developed and fine-tuned themselves.

They found new tastes. And it kept on developing, right up until the end; his descent from grace—from the roof of the block of flats.

THE FALLEN BOY'S FRIEND:

Mikey went to Salford and Greater Manchester for the music and bands. However, most that went to that College and halls had a shitty mix of CDs. It amazed him just how shitty: Simply-bastard-Red next to the Lightning-shithouse-Seeds next to Guns N' Fucking-Roses.

Some fellow students stood out though. And they all had at least one album: 'Definitely Maybe'. And, these were true stars. Those that had this and the first Stone Roses album. You could filter the tossers from people worth talking to using this all as a dipstick. The public school boys might have 'walked the school leopard', played 'Soggy Biscuit' and got a Henry hoover stuck to their dicks, but, by College and having stayed in those flats, their shirts went from tucked in, to hanging out. The music did that.

It wasn't long before Billy and Mikey were drinking in the Black Horse and Woolpack with the rest of them. By 'rest of them', Mikey's brain meant the 'real' locals. These were the actual people the songs on the CDs they had were made from; true grit, so to speak.

Mikey gave himself short-lived food poisoning cooking sausages for the first time on the first night. And, Billy gave him a spliff to get over it. From then on they were friends, albeit from the opposite ends of the social ladder. Mikey didn't care, his new pet working-class monkey had depth and kept his boarding school cling-ons at a distance. Last thing he wanted was another porn mag' rammed under his door before his folks came to visit—great public school joke that was. Mikey used to pass out at parties. This made him a target by the same tossers he was trying to create a distance from. And… he got sick of waiting for his eyebrows to grow back.

It took Mikey a while to get Billy out of his room. Sometimes he could hear a girl's voice in there, sometimes a guitar, sometimes both. But, it was when it was silent, and he knew he was in there—that's when it really rattled him. The silence was there but he could feel a definite presence.

When some chavs tried to mug them both on their walk to college one morning, he gave them a couple of fags to get rid of them. Mikey was actually more scared of what Billy would do to them if he didn't. He knew they'd all had a lucky escape. By then the darkness had set into the flats, and into Billy, and this girl he was seeing at the time.

Mikey could see it and had to move out in the end. The flats had got to him too; spooked him out. He wasn't meant for all that weird shit that was going on.

He left Billy to it and never heard from him again. He'd driven off before the intro' to I Wanna be Adored had finished.

His heart sank, and he was sick, when he read what had happened in the papers. It was a sickness far worse than when he'd eaten those half-defrosted sausages of horse lips and arseholes. No, this was real primal sickness. At life and what it can do to people. He asked himself why he hadn't taken Billy with him, forced him to see one more band, to go to another club night. Mikey could get pinned up against the wall by a big bird again, a Russian shot putter type that wanted to have him. Billy always liked that. He used to laugh back then... sometimes.

Why did he have to do it? The stupid sod. Why did he jump from the flats?

HE TRIED, BUT at first... he couldn't remember the last time he'd seen a smile from him. Then it occurred to him. Billy had done something weird. Mikey had forgotten about it until now. As the newspaper showing Billy's 'suicide' was spread out in front of him it came to him. The last time he saw him smile, in fact had seen him... at all.

He was helping Mikey pack up the car to leave. As Billy had closed the car door, his finger was inside of it. Intentionally, it seemed now. As Mikey started the engine Billy lifted a slightly bloody hand up and blew a kiss to Mikey.

Mikey remembered now; those drips of blood from Billy's hand. He had blocked it out, as he put The Stone Roses on the car stereo, and drove off.

In the mirror, Mikey saw him smile.

And that was it—the last time. Now he was gone. The fragile complicated pieces of him smashed into the same piece of earth beneath those flats where the bloody drops had hit.

They'd never be back together again. Billy was gone for good—dead.

2

Dice Man

I TOOK THE fallen boy's case:
I'd been writing all the while. Automatic now. It helped me process past pains and possibilities of a future. She was right about that, my therapist. One of several women that pulled at the strings of my making. Another was a mixed-up copper: Cherry. A real master puppeteer that one. And then the third that made up the holy trinity was E. L. Noire. An ex-burlesque dancer; stage name: M. Pampelmousse. Now she was a barmaid and an accidental literary agent. She came across a lot of dark and dirty tales working behind the bar of The Hatchet Inn. And she came across mine.

A DRUNK'S CLENCHED limp cock sprayed up against the other side of the glass phone box. A patchwork of faded and ripped flyers of propositions splattered around the shelf I'd put my notebook on, all scrawled, printed, copied and stuck. They all came with similar offers: money for sex and sex for money… That, less money, meant the less you'd get. And, that with more money, the luckier you'd get. It was hard to digest with the smell, stains and tainted texture of the handset. I gripped it hard and looked to Manchester and a case to take me there.

I'd decided to make my own luck. Like some Dice Man experiment I called Directory Enquiries and asked for a bingo hall near to my target:

'Hello John, Gala Bingo, in Pendleton… Are you still there?' she asked and I realised I'd drifted into a familiar hole; dreaming myself into another place. A pit. Her words snapped me to.

'Yes, I'm still here. I'm John Barrie, I'm investigating a case and it's imperative that I speak to whoever's calling the balls out. Now.'

Why hadn't I thought on my feet quicker, made a name up better than that one?! Why still use that name…the one the police gave me to use?

I'd already decided I'd take my real name back to Manchester. It would be whispered on corners and in the shadows: 'John Black. He's back…' With that I was sure they'd come for me; to silence me, break and bury or drown me in the canals for everything I'd said in court. And I'd have my chance.

I'd be ready for the perpetual hate machines. My name could silence a noisy pub, the needle would stop, pints would fall and the air would thicken. I was all for the drama whilst still in control of my destiny.

'BALL CALLER? That's Si… I mean Simon.' 'Yes, I need to speak to Simon—it's urgent.'

'I think he's in the middle of a game, sir. Hundreds of purple rinses looking at him right now. Waiting to top up their pension with this week's bonus ball.'

'That's why I'm calling; I have to catch him before it finishes. Simon…now…please?!'

'…let me try,' she said.

I felt some sort of guilt at using the words *investigating*, *urgent* and *now*. It wasn't—not for them.

Finding this case might as well have been with the flip of a coin or a set of darts thrown behind me at a map whilst blindfolded. I was gambling with a city and the people in it—it's all connected. It always is. I felt it rolling; both the imagined dice and the actual piss from another drunk on the other side of the glass. It trickled, almost in slow motion. It went over where the glass stopped short at the bottom of the phone box and over my shoes. I sneered at him. I went to take my cock out and piss right back at him. Shocked it would seem by the apparent wall he was pissing against animating and coming to life, he was gone.

'I'll put you through now. We'll have to be quick,' she said and I waited for the click.

'Click.'

'Hello, Simon Speaking, Simon England. This'd better be good. And real fucking urgent.'

'Hello Simon. John Barrie here. I'm working on a case. I need your help.'

'Can't it wait?'

'The time is now Simon, NOW,' I stated and looked back at my notebook and my piss covered shoes.

I re-read: I was reborn into this on my 27th Birthday. So, 27. I'd use that.

'27 SIMON.'

'What?'

'Number 27—have you called it?'

'I don't understand…' he sounded confused. I was too. But sometimes you just gotta roll with it.

'It's very important Simon. You think you don't have any time. Look around you. Look at the old eyes and mouths with fags hanging out; all beading at you now. How much time do

you think they've got?' and I paused for it to sink in, 'Now…
the number 27 Simon…'

'Yes, I've called it,' he answered. Then came a change in tone:
suspicious. Maybe he thought it was a wind-up. Maybe he
smelled the drink on my breath down the line, maybe he saw me
down that phone line; covered in drunk's piss and standing in
the rain of a Bristol phone box.

I'd summoned almost all the residual confidence I had to
throw at him.

'27… Recently. You're sure you've pulled it out?'

'Duck and a Crutch—yeah sure, at the end of the last card.'
'Now listen very carefully, lives will depend on it,' and the cliché
stung my lips. I shook my head in disgust, 'The last people to
get 27 on their cards, to tick it off,' *just like me*, I thought, *my 27th
year—tick, done*. 'I need to speak to them, it's an investigation.
Pretty please. Go fuckin' get em!'

'Erh, right. O.K., wait,' he puzzled and spurted the words out
as his brain was thrown a curveball—his routine shaken up by
my confidently delivered madness.

I heard him put the phone to one side in a single fluid motion.
A thud followed. Then feedback from the microphone. He went
back to address his crowd and as he did I imagined the faces,
the smoke, the high ceiling, the parked-up mobility scooters
around the sides. I saw the pints on tables, and I saw their
husbands and other halves and partners in their own respective
pubs, bars, alone at home, or in the bath or at the races. That, or
further detached and 6ft under.

'Ladies and gentlemen, sorry to interrupt…' he announced
and I heard laughter in the background.

'There's no gentlemen 'ere love. Just you—if you see any
though, point 'em out!' a voice shouted.

'Yeah could do with a gentleman,' another went. Then came

more laughter. Layered on top of a drum of chatter.

'Not so gentle though eh?! Yeah not too soft either, I could do with a real hard...' the original voice continued but was cut short.

'Ladies, ladies... I've the police on the line... It's important. They just need some help then we can get back on with the game.'

'FUCK da police!' a united mass shouted. Then it all went silent for a moment, before erupting again as they laughed it off. 'I don't think they want to speak to you,' Simon said timidly, caught between a rock and a hard place. And having temporarily

shifted himself back to the phone for cover.

'I'm NOT the police. It's important. The number 27s! I have to speak to them,' I insisted and there was a pause. With it came a tension feeling him deciding whether to put the phone down and finish it. Or, was he to push and challenge me: why am I asking this, and why exactly I needed the 27ers?

'Ladies. The last of you to strike off 27. To the desk. This gentleman—not the police. He urgently needs to speak to you,' and his voice and feedback echoed down the lines and across the Bingo hall. He took the easy option; passed the buck back to me. 'Good luck fella, they're coming up to the desk now. They look pissed—in every sense... wait... there, here... you've five 27ers now... Good luck pal,' and he stepped aside giving the handset to someone on the other end.

'Yes?' a curt voice came. I only knew it was female because I'd been told that's all there was in the hall. Rough as old nails; a Marlboro-sandpaper throat mix spewed down the phone at me.

'I'm calling about the case.' 'What case?'

'Next...' I said.

'Hello?' another non-gendered noise bit and barked at me down the line.

'I'm calling about the case.' 'What case?'

'Next...'

'Hello, can I help?' went a slightly less cutting noise. This one slightly more defrosted but not totally thawed out as it met mine over the handset.

'I'm calling about the case.'

'What? Will's case? Billy-boy?' and the voice softened some. I thought: third time's a charm. If that charm is a rasped North-Western accent wrapped around an old bag of smashed crabs.

'Yes, Will's case. Are you the right person to talk to?'

'No, it's Nancy's boy. She's behind me here. Thought it was done with ages ago. Police closed it up. Whatever-the-fuck they know.' she said. I felt the sympathy in her voice for this Nancy girl as much as the hatred for the authorities.

I'm not the police. She thought I was phoning to help her friend so why wouldn't she thaw out, melt back down and give me a chance knowing I wasn't one of them? It was familiar ground now. Filling in where they couldn't.

'Hello... You're calling about Will, my Son? The police said they couldn't do anymore. T'was Suicide they said,' a voice quivered, 'Will B. Rowes; my son... Billy to us. I'm Nancy. Nancy Rowes.' And it was as if everyone else in the room, my formula and equation, and the rabble had all dissolved into the background as she spoke. A grave situation had emerged and the world fell back to black. Just the two of us; whispering tender, fragile words to a tender audience in each other:

'Don't say any more Nancy, I want to help. I'm a P.I. If there's anything more to it... I can and will find out. To put your mind to rest, for good. I've access to everything the police have. That, and everything they can't get to. The stuff they won't and daren't touch—eve-ry-thing! I won't stop until the job's done—you understand Nancy?' I said it and I meant it.

In the time she spoke I omitted any thoughts of the giant beasts of my past in that city. The ones that would want to join the party from the surrounding ganglands as soon as they heard I was back there. Come one, come all. And like my first case, when I was done, she'd have answers and my enemies would be forgotten or I'd be done or dead; buried or floating face down in the canal.

No longer bothered by memories of them, I tried to invent a future for myself. That all seemed good reasoning at the time. Besides, I thought: Manchester had some good pubs. Good, dark, nasty little holes to squeeze into with sweat dripping down the walls as you stretch to the bar. With the music of great apes banging at you through speakers as your back pocket is picked. Yes, Manchester had some great holes to hide-up in. I would have a welcome home party in every one of them, whilst solving this case for Nancy. Fucking the demons of my past in the ass— that would be a sideshow.

'If you want my help, Nancy, don't say any more. Think about it. Then send me the details, to this address…' and I left it with her, put the receiver down, and picked up my notebook. I snapped the red elastic around it: 'crack'.

I STEPPED OUT into what was left of the piss and rain and looked into the dark skies above the phone box. I thought, I waited and then I walked on.

Now, I had the case to take me to Manchester. So the ghosts of my past would quit eating me to the bone where I lay. I'd take the fight to them.

NANCY'S NOTES ARRIVED on my fourth day, fourth

hangover, and second meal of the week. When the A4 envelope drifted down to the pile of ignored mail, I had to remind myself why I was seeing it.

It glared up at me like the last chance to pull myself up and out of the hole I'd put myself in. Like a beacon calling me to my next chapter, a battle or gutter to slump into. And then the true point of it came back to me…because if I wasn't on a case, this case, I was just a drunken writer without any material outside of my own skin. The flat and the wood-chipped wallpaper in it wasn't much of a sane resting place. My purpose was in the envelope. It was a distraction and a means to an abstraction of myself; a move away from the spectres, the bars, the bottles and piss-troughs of this town—opening up the door to my demons elsewhere.

I re-focussed, packed, and headed for Temple Meads train station. I didn't need much; it was in me all that I needed for the days that would follow: the memories of fights, wars, scuffles, and those hard beatings given and taken. Those memories, deep in my flesh, under my skin and underneath my nails—that shit didn't come off.

THE CITY WOULD feel my second coming:

When I arrive in Manchester and walk through Piccadilly Gardens the flowers would blacken. The grass would die. Resting punks on the benches would look on through hollow eyes. Then they'd look to the ground as cracks crumble through the pavement under our feet. As I worked the streets, and battled upstream against the city's undercurrents.

3

Slide Away

Saturday, Midday:

TEMPLE MEADS STATION rose up on the horizon like a Victorian Castle. Brunel's node of the South West which still draws Londoners and the Welsh to a Graveyard of content: the City of Bristol.

The path ramped up and seemed to pull on the black holdall I shouldered. People rushed past as a multi-coloured blur, clambering, running late to catch their trains. I walked my own pace, alone—I cut through them all.

She was at the top of the ramp, blocking the main entrance. My prior trial by fire: the fiery-haired femme fatale, Cherry. An undercover policewoman. She'd played me before—she'd played me good. Previously, she'd been the only one ever really in control, as she pulled my strings, lit my fuse. I'd been a walking, battering, drinking, explosive mess. She made it so I'd exploded at all the right pressure points and her jobs were done. For her. For the police.

It wasn't that long ago I'd seen her, her pants were still under my bed. But she was here again, now on a professional level. The case wasn't theirs though. I'd created this one myself.

BEFORE I REACHED her at th top of the ramp, I opened the top of the holdall and took out the envelope. It'd been opened already, cello-taped back shut—of course, it had. I ripped at it and scanned the contents. They'd seen it already, added some pieces. My heart and gut dropped at another played out game where the rules and set-pieces had been messed with, all before I'd even stepped up to the plate.

'Our protection stops when you leave the platform,' she said and handed me a tiny suppository of a mobile phone and tickets for the train. Her words reached out to me, not as a threat, or warning. More as a tease and suggestion of me being let loose and untethered again; off the leash—like a fierce dog with a lockjaw, unable to give up the bait.

She smiled and I returned it best I could; out of practice with my growing emotions. She'd been my controller, lover, friend and confidant. How much and in what proportions I couldn't be sure because of a fog clouding it all. I knew now she'd added strength to me that overrode the insecurities.

I put a rolled cigarette up to my lips, she lit it, and we walked into the station together. The train waited at the platform and four officers faced us equally spaced apart; their feet spread, like a black and white barrier.

'He's being let out,' she said gravely. And it was obvious who she meant, 'There'll be more of his lot waiting to welcome him when he gets out too. They'll be on the streets in a few days, probably three at most,'her words: another deadline to me.

She was referring to the gangland boss I'd testified against in Manchester. The case resulted in me being put on witness protection in Bristol. She'd said it, knowing it wouldn't stop me clearly. She'd felt she should say it regardless, knowing I would go anyway. Maybe he was just another police mess for me to tidy up behind them.

'A rival clan will probably have a pop at him before you get close, or make yourself felt... I just thought you should know.'

'It'll make what I have to do easier… You want me to finish what you've all started and can't bury…again. That's why
  you're really telling me isn't it?'

'Yes,' she said and tears welled up in her big green eyes.

We hadn't had what you'd call a conventional relationship to date. This was the first obvious sign. She'd shown me her vulnerabilities. It was a beautiful contrast to the stoic strength she'd shown up until now. There we were, like real everyday people. Just the two of us, saying goodbye on the platform; hugging, kissing, crying, missing each other before the train departed with me on it to pull us apart.

A solitary lone-tear made it past the lashes and rolled down a cheek. And in it, I saw a life, a future, and dreams of future memories where we might have had something. Something close to one of those conventional lives; walks on the beach, coffees in the sun outside cafés, holding hands. And then the tear rolled over those lips. It dropped slowly from her chin to the concrete platform below. A splash of dust and a fragile love came up in those particles. Her look glazed over. Her gaze returned back to those stony-strong eyes I knew; focussed… and on the target.

As were mine. They were never changed.

My destination was a hell; made of my past. I was as drawn by the badness, as it was to me.

'YOU'RE HARDER THAN that. Listen… You know what I have to do. Always had to…so I can move on. Besides I've another job to do there,' and I tapped the bag with the envelope on top, 'The one where you lot took it as far as you could, again, before it got to lines you couldn't cross. And people you couldn't touch. That's where I come in. Wading through the shit so you don't stain your uniforms,'

'You should have been a poet,' she said sarcastically.

'And you should have been a police officer,' I cracked back. My words gestured at her unconventional way she had at working the force. I backed her up with a dig at my writing that followed: 'you've read my notes and the last lot. Poetry doesn't come into it...'

The whistle blew in the background.

A girl with a short skirt rushed past. I half smiled at Cherry, as my eyes followed the passing skirt as it rode high as the girl boarded with a flash of thigh. I went to board, distracted. I missed the step up to the carriage and scraped the full length of my shin on the edge of the iron step. The pain could have awoken a Kraken... And, so it did as I opened wide to the shame of it and made a silent scream.

'You deserve that John Barrie!' she taunted.

'Black... It's John Black,' I stated, cold and closed the door. I saw her face change through the glass. It turned to fear at the sound of my real name. It hit her square in the face and blunt; my carelessness having said it out loud. Her fears came at the suggestion I was gonna take my real name back to Manchester and Salford, without making any attempt to hide it. No more hiding behind the one they gave me in Bristol, and the façade they built around me.

The FEAR: Forget, Everything And Re-attack... The FEAR: As I Forget Everything And yet I can't help but Remember. Before the train hits Piccadilly station, I'd remember and regroup inside of myself: primed.

THE OFFICERS TURNED to face the train as my carriage passed them. They nodded at me out of some sort of respect, and I toasted them back with a can from my bag. The last ones shook their heads slowly as I lifted it slowly to my lips. I smiled as the train moved on and out. Its speed built—an unstoppable force taking me to the end of my line… As long as there wasn't a leaf, cow, or a discarded jumper on the track.

'Clack…clack' 'Clack…clack' 'Clack…clack'

'PSST…' And I opened the second can before we'd reached the first stop. It was going to be a long ride.

I opened the brown envelope, dropped the contents to the flip-down table in front of me. Placing the tiny mobile phone and my black notebook alongside, I picked up the envelope's guts to read.

First, I looked for any interference by the Police, Cherry, and any other forces that may be out there to fuck with me. There was a letter and some photos with a newspaper clipping fastened to the top. It was from the old dear in the Bingo hall: Nancy. This was the first piece I'd scan read on the ramp-up to Temple Meads. And then there was the second couple of A4s of paper clipped together.

The first, an extra sheet and predictably with a police letterhead. It was to the point, listed out, succinct:

John,

We've got you a job on security in the block of flats—where he jumped. It comes with a shitty flat. You can't forget to put the seat down there—it doesn't have one.

And the local is full of ex-gangster pissheads. All has- been-wash-ups. You'll fit right in.

Signed: Cherry X

The second sheet was on thick cotton paper with beautiful

handwritten calligraphy in a rich deep blue ink. The words filled the page, entwined together with an illustration and something more than just words and drawings. A small blue bird flapped on the outskirts sketched as if having dropped the words. It was from my accidental literary agent; the burlesque beauty from the 70s.

From the desk of E. L. Noire:

Drink enough to write and to stay alive. No more. No less.
This isn't a journey's end. It's a crack at a new beginning.
Send your notes, when you're done – You dirt-bag!
Come back to me. Love, lust, empathy,
Mademoiselle Pampelmousse XXX

On the other side of the aisle, there was a table of four. They all looked familiar, but not a threat. I recognised them, meanwhile, I was invisible to them. It was better that way. Ignored them for now and returned to the case; Nancy's notes, her heart, soul and her worries about her Son:

Pushed, she thinks. Jumped, the police say. Bigger picture covered up, I thought.

I re-read everything. I looked at the press clippings. And a sorry photo of the boy at what looked like a family caravan holiday. In it, he was perched at a compact table holding a can of Budweiser. The rain and darkness loomed outside behind him and made the caravan interior, him and the camera holder feel futile. All seemed about to be crushed around them by nature's embrace of the can they were in. It must have been in Scotland. The look in his eyes was that of caring little at the situation and those in front of him. Instead he is more focussed on drinking past whatever forced family occasion has him trapped: the weather-beaten caravan photo shoot. His feigned smile seals it.

There's no real clue as to when it was taken, and the real darkness that lay ahead of him... To that fall, jump, being pushed, or the leap fourteen stories down to the tarmac that shattered his future. His mother's heart went over the edge too, down and hard into that unsympathetic floor below.

It always rained in Manchester. As it was in the next photos I picked up. It was the crime scene shots—he was on the floor. It was captured in the creased news clipping too, the moments after he made contact with the tarmac below the block of flats. The rain had washed away most of the blood and skull of the boy, but everything else remained. They could demolish the whole site of the block of flats but the essence of the events would stay behind.

The police couldn't be trusted in the boy's case. Unless a verdict the public and family were happy with was released—his mother wouldn't rest. That was clear in Nancy's words over the phone: 'T'was Suicide they said.' But there was 'pushed', 'persuaded' and 'it wasn't like him' in the undercurrents and subtext of the words she didn't say. The words she didn't need to. The roaring mass around had sounded: 'Fuck the Police'. It resonated again in these words in front of me. Best I could do was dig around in the undergrowth for the facts, share them. From me, she might accept a verdict and be able to sleep a little at night—win her Bingo card, love her lost boy, and move on. The rain would still come each day, but it would feel a little lighter on her shoulders.

Sitting back to think, I drained the last can. Delivered straight to my stomach, I wasn't even aware of swallowing.

Looking over, the group of four were in tune, full of banter, and a hundred miles an hour nattering to each other. Scottish, I thought. Their words overlapped, merged, blended and washed all around. Occasionally there was a peak, a shout, laugh, and swear word accompanied by a bang on the table. I was unnerved by their familiarity.

Where did I know them from?

A young girl walked down the aisle. She stopped, looked at me then back at them. She hesitated—in complete awe.

'Can I...do you... mind?' she said nervously. Her hands shook while holding a notebook and pen. Apparently she was looking at me for some sort of permission. I felt confused. Complemented and bemused, I reached out to take the pen from her. She then snapped them away, turned to the table of four, and asked for autographs. They immediately sobered up— real pros. Still drunk...true professionals—professionally wasted. It looked to be part of their personas, well-crafted and worn like their Adidas three stripes.

There was some; 'I love you guys,' from her and they returned with smiles, half hugs and taps on her shoulder. Another three or four fans passed, all girls, each looking to me first as if to ask permission, and then turned to the table opposite. By the fifth autograph hunter I realised with my demeanour, black outfit, papers on the table in front of me and correlating fill of beer, I must have looked like a manager, a hanger-on or some random admin' bag carrying idiot.

I picked up my things and moved to the buffet car, and another round.

LEANING AGAINST THE small window shelf, I saw the world as it moved past like a hurried Monet painting. It dripped nature's colours sideways. Occasional fence lines, houses, trees and posts flickered by; changing the composition. It blacked out with tunnels and each passing train. Each time it returned; rushing to force nature's palette onto the canvas of my eye.

'Clack…clack.' 'Clack…clack.' 'PSSST.'

'Black's back,'

I started to imagine the words from the tracks' voice.

And then it came to me, where I felt I knew them; the table of four. It hit me as the chemical memories rose from a forgotten pit in my mind:

One…was the bassist from a band I once loved. And I would do again as soon as I neared the homeland of the beat where he had once played. As soon as I entered Manchester. As the smoke of the factories stung at my nose. He was in *that* band once. Now, he's in another. When I worked the door of the club I'd pinched his girl's thigh or arse and he'd faced me off on the dance floor. Rightly so. A mistake on my behalf as I didn't see anyone with her; certainly not him. You couldn't hear a word in the club so introducing yourself required a touch, a squeeze, a glance. Or, bypassing that; to go in for a kiss. Luckily, I had gone for a light touch…of sorts. And, that I had then backed down. I knew his label and he pretty much owned the place at the time, and with it; they owned me too. I remembered my surprise at seeing him there as she had moved to one side in a flash of the lights, strobes and smoke. I had diffused it all with a look. He could see worship in my eyes. Lucky for me and him as his music sounded better with his fingers still intact. There were more important things than one woman's arse at stake; his beat moved the hips of a generation. I wouldn't miss that for a strobe hidden grope behind the striped pillars of that club. Everything was spoken for, owned, and coded in there. Her arse was probably catalogued somewhere too; a butt that many had decoded, but not me. Not that night.

Back then the club would soon close, driven by events I'd

been involved in, the court case, a young girl's fall and my failed attempt to rescue her that night.

A night that had insisted on taking her from the world. Eventually, after a slight respite and return it would close for good. Fittings, fixtures and even the urinals would be auctioned off. It would be replaced by flats and a nondescript plaque. But ambassadors, like this musician and the rest of them would live on, on tape, vinyl, CDs. They would float around in the city's veins, the canals, remaining factories and the record stores and live forever – feeding us the past, the music that bound us; its love spreads.

The drunken ruminations momentarily lifted.

MY TRAIN TICKETS were checked and stamped as I looked out of the window. I looked for things that weren't there. My mind mapped over the morphing horizons behind the glass. My eyes tried to stitch them together into ever-changing scenes.

It was three or four cans before we had to change trains at Birmingham; I didn't know exactly just how many. It felt right, the number and amount; the liquid backbone I needed to step foot off the train. I meant to be drunk by the time I reached my old battlefield that was my journey's end.

At Birmingham, the claustrophobia of the city, the station and the mass of people were too much and I was relieved to be boarding another train and leave it behind. It felt wrong to its core, like visiting the murder scene of a dead relative or a mass family grave. Or, maybe it was just too far away from the sea and the waters. The ones that once washed away the pains that anchored me. They had soothed, remade and birthed me. Where the Viking-warrior of my past-heritage came together with me as one.

I re-boarded and the metal can on the track that carried rock stars, fans, a drunk writer and private eye pushed on towards Manchester. With it loomed the inevitable confrontations. Life's pain, love and music was ready to rush at me. I was ready. I'd reach out to grasp the stinging nettle with both hands. Moving headlong into it all again I was still standing, leaning, drinking and trying to figure it all out for someone else's greater good. This time it was for Nancy and her boy.

Fallen, pushed or jumped?

'Clack…clack.'

I would keep moving, change and purge my past, if I could survive it—going against the mob boss. Mr Big himself now he was to be released.

'Clack…clack.'

In the end, maybe, it would actually have been for someone else though. As that tear had settled, drying into the station platform I had left behind—maybe it was all for her; Cherry.

'Clack…clack.'

My agent too, E.L. Noire…and of course for my therapist who always got to read into my mind. When she was done… They'd all have had their pound of flesh.

'Clack…clack.'

For all of them, and for Nancy's boy. 'Clack…clack.'

'Black's…back.'

4

Made of Stone

MOTHER-MANCHESTER SWALLOWED the train with a blanket of grey. Rain and the smog of industry, breweries and relentless traffic were all around. With no gradual build-up of population, houses and industrial units to the city, it just happened; it was there. Everywhere. Its presence hit me out of the blue like a brick in the face thrown from its many factory walls. I'd been there before, travelled that line, entered it many times. Each time I still got the same awakening, eyes opening; a realisation to the endless brick. And the dank soup of it all.

Despite this, it had a gravitas. Like a charming old man. And a fierce stone maze too—with hidden demons around each corner.

It was familiar enough to take for granted. You could vanish forever, and find your fate in those canals; forever forgotten amongst the veins flowing past the wastelands and the derelict industrial shells.

It felt bleak as hell. It was good to be back.

The train shuddered to a stop and I nearly fell opening the door. I steadied myself on the bar on the inside and ledge that had been my journey's steadying companion.

THE ARMED POLICE in line on the platform wasn't a surprise. I walked through them. A nod to the first and last. They didn't return much. I was nothing to them or worse I was a walking inconvenience. A disaster waiting to happen. If they acknowledged my return they might take responsibility for my actions. They knew I was off the official radar for sure.

I didn't have many friends to welcome me back. I wouldn't make any either.

Cherry had said *he*, Mr Big, would be out in a few days. Something hadn't gone to plan in the court—I was there to make things right on the street. It suited this dirty old town that had missed me really, to face it head-on.

First, I headed for the Northern Quarter. The place I headed for was the sister bar to a club. The one at the heart of all this dark shit that surrounded me. I should have stayed away from it. I could have just focussed on Nancy's case from a distance, and skirted around the edges; spying, crawling around and eavesdropping on my demons.

It wasn't my style. A few drinks in, I was feeling reckless.

I aimed to sit in that bar, make some early notes and think out Nancy's case. As I did, the bar and everyone in it would know I'd arrived. The message would be out there. And whilst I tried to fix Nancy's mind over how her boy hit the ground, from fourteen stories up, the criminal scum would hear of my return. It'd save me the effort of fishing them out—instead, they'd come to me.

I walked through Piccadilly Gardens. Passing a mass of overflowing bins, cans, concrete, intersection of tram lines and drunken punks—out of their generation; wasted on the benches.

I turned down Oldham St, passed Sacha's Hotel, where parts of an old story resonated in my head:

A dildo rolling out from under a footballer's bed after they'd realised their wallet had been taken... And the scars the team had left on a girl

that would never be made right. Not anywhere near closed-up and made
easier by the contents of the wallet she'd stolen.

My memory was in pieces. It was a reminder of the hive
mentality that worked through every tier here, waiting to bite
out. You could float around Bristol in a half-stoned daze.
Manchester, however, was a different beast—you had to work
at it. Or, it could wear you down. Even the trees looked
aggressive, bare and ready to stab out. I passed Affleck's Palace,
feet aching and I realised the scale of the city is often forgotten. I
made it a few blocks and my soles burned as my black holdall
swung and my body sunk into the concrete slabs below.

On cue, it started to rain. Heavy, treacle-like and with a
darkness only it could create in the North-West of England.
Despite being only a few yards from the black canopy outside
of the bar I was drenched by the time I crossed the road and
darted into it. There was a barrier of sorts barricading some
seating outside. Yellow and black striped pillars triggered
another flashback: a girl falling from the stage, her blood and
the ignorant revellers around her.

That was the incident. The one that had made it all too much
for me. I took a stand against it all in court, in my life and now…
I was back; standing against it again.

IT WAS TIME: I took aim and went to take another dose from
mother-Manchester's teats.

My shoes echoed across the concrete floor of the Industrial
shell of the place. I leant against the bar like I owned it. The
barman's back was to me. He cleared up the broken remains of
a huge mirror. A list of barred punters was stuck to the only
corner of it that remained.

As he turned, I dropped my bag to the floor. I looked up to see the mirror wasn't the only thing to take a beating. His blackened eye and split lip looked fresh.

I was in for a life story before I got my drink:

'How was I to know he fucking owned the place. Or his record label does,' he started.

'Pint.' I injected and as I did he moved towards the pump between us.

'Seriously, what the fuck?!' And he shook, giving the drip tray a shameful look.

'Kept your job though,' I reminded him.

'I don't know yet, he hasn't been back in. Fucker winged a bottle at my head. Mirror exploded. Most punters thought a gun had gone off,' and he waved behind himself at the damaged bottles of Jack Daniels added to the list of casualties.

'You'll be alright, no one owns shit. They all belong to the city, and you do too. His band, the label, this bar—all of it. It's a church and you're one of the reluctant priests.' I thanked him with a toast, and took the pint and drank it straight down a third.

I read the 'barred list' behind him. It'd been partially printed then scribbled over in pen and pencil over and over again.

A mix of manic varied handwriting tempos showcased the many altercations, all highlighted with stains of blood and splashed drinks—a lasting testament to the place in a peak of activity.

It read…

STILL BARRED

PRETEND DEAF GUY (*point and shout—he can definitely hear, just not 'last orders' or to 'stop hitting kids'*).

BLACKY TWO WATCHES *(on each wrist—actually has four watches in total. And he isn't black—it's dirt—wears a big parker all the time, think he's packing too.*
Tread careful... call the firm).

GINGER CUNT *(there's a few, this one's a 6ft fucker... Just don't let any ginges in except Mick—He'll probably be in his own place anyway. Champagne charlie M'Fucker!).*

CRAZY BLONDE! *(catches pints on stage between her giraffe-like legs).*

BILL & GREASY STEW *(They're o.k. on their own... might bore people to death though so chuck em' owt anyway! Wash ya hands after, or you'll be dropping the glasses all night).*

THAT 80s CHAV *(NOT Shaun, let him in—he owns the place!!).*

'SCRAPPER' IN SHELL SUIT—*It's half-burnt now after 'last time', he still wears it... Still smokes too! Crazy bastard. Spare fire extinguishers behind the bar—Use the drip trays first.*

B.O. BARACASS *(use the stick behind the bar to cattle-prod him outa the place...he MINGS!!!).*

CHINA BOB *(don't confront this fucker—call the Firm or Industry. Unless he's sat or stood with the Firm or Industry—leave well alone—and look fucking busy!!).*

HELL-ON *(Toilet Bomber. If she's been—get her to*

clean up first before chucking 'er out).

JOHN BLACK *(Call the firm. He wears all black too, and camo jacket – see photo!! Nobody's friend.*
Everybody's enemy now. Fucker got the club closed over that mess with the O-D-ing girl).

CHINASKI or FANTE or RAYMOND *(Don't waste any time on these lot).*

BRIAN SHRYMP-TOWN *(Check his pockets for drugs at the start of the night, then sell back to him later on*
— often seen with J. Black… Sell them a few drinks first
though—they can drink… a lot…and we need the money).

I didn't care that my name was on the list, it was why I'd dropped in—to send a message.

'You going to add him to the list?' I joked about whoever had bust the mirror and blackened his eye.

'I should, the cunt. You in town long? I'm Dylan, what's your name anyway?' he said, just small talk, no point or feeling behind it. He looked to the near vacant empty bar that was behind me, except for the shadows and the back of a lone drinker or two.

'I'm John… John Black… Third from the bottom on that list,' I necked the pint and pointed. I picked up my bag and left. It was dead in there and I'd touched base enough; left a message… I focussed on the true calling, the case, the notes; Nancy's fallen boy.

Outside, what was left of the rain dripped from the bar's canopy to my head. Three lads in tracksuits barged past me, walking like apes. Their arms swung, carrying invisible dumbbells that weighed them down—true Mancs. A Northern-chav-fury possessed them and the last in line shoulder barged me on his way through.

They turned in unison.

Arms covered their faces and they started hopping on the spot. A well-rehearsed and clichéd confrontation starter. I'd seen this routine before, all too much.

'What-cha cunt,' one seethed through gritted teeth, 'what's your fuckin' problem?!' they added.

They looked like three underweight boxers warming up and bobbing about on the spot. It was an ugly feeble show of strength. My inaction and stare nudged their movement out of sync. I knew I had them. I looked down, picked a ready rolled cigarette out of my coat pocket, brought it slowly to my lips. I lit it and looked back up. Real slow. I looked through the first in line to a horizon behind him.

'I am a cunt,' I said, cold and gritted, as I continued to look straight through all of them. It was through to the wars, blood, flesh and tears I'd seen in this city and overseas—these three were mere stains to me. I drew heavily on the cigarette, and my past, and then I let the bag drop to the floor. An exclamation to what was to come. It fell from my shoulder to the wet pavement and I placed my hands calmly to my sides; poised, charged, loaded.

The lads had lost their rhythm and looked uncertain. They were rattled, but all of them were too proud to be the first to back off.

A phone rang in the bar behind me and then the door opened. 'It's for you. The Firm, they want a word,' the barman said as a matter of fact…ice-cold words. His message was delivered

and he knew the weight of it.

The tracksuits disappeared back into the piss, wind and streets that they came from; off to try and mug some other poor bastard. My demeanour had shaken them and at the mention of the Firm, it was the final straw. All too heavy for the lightweights.

I about-turned and walked to the end of the bar. A black old handset was off the hook. I picked it straight up:

'You don't waste any time. You're not even out yet.' I said, knowing who was on the other end.

'You fucked us son,' a grave voice both confessed, and accused me from the other end of the line. 'Fucked the place over too. They'll knock it down and turn it into fucking flats. Do you know how many people keep coming for the place? And the bands, the music, the DJs...'

'Drugs too...' I butted in.

'Don't start, you self-righteous prick. Wasn't our fault she couldn't handle it. With everything you've done, seen and been through. Some wasted bitch touched your moral nerve did she? She was fucking nothing... NOTH...ING. Just some heroin-chic looking bitch that took a gammy E and drank too much water. She was fuck-all, and now you are too Black. You're going to join her. The club's on its last legs. You robbed the city of its heart. You're done Jacky boy... John. We're coming for you. That's if the city doesn't do you in first. There's no love for you anymore. You've had it. You tore it apart.'

I let him say his piece, pausing long enough to build atmosphere. Fear and tension in a suggested uncertainty.

'You hired me...knew my background. You should know better than to throw threats around,' and I paused again, took a pint glass from behind the bar, put it under the nearest tap and poured one out. 'I'll be seeing you.'

I finished, and hung up.

'Tastes like piss,' I said to the barman who'd been watching and listening all the while.

I left the unfinished pint behind on the bar, picked up the black holdall.

This time, I left for good.

5

Bitter Sweet Symphony

PUSHED ON BY a beer-fed, bullet-proof feeling jacket, I floated across the pavements and streets.

There was something to the city's essence, even within the threats, weather and attempted mugging, it felt even more like home. A false sense of security maybe, and a love of the dank, dark brutality of the place. It always came through. With each step the city touched my already tainted heart. It came in the air from the breweries I breathed, and in the stained bombed cracked pavements I walked over—again and again it all came back to me.

Mr. Big's call had reached out from his lair, a cell or his mother's living room. His evil filled tendrils were woven throughout the fabric of the city. His poison seeped out of the city's shadows, cracks and pores.

I'd felt the static between me, the city and the people. It was even in the city's degenerate walls. Everything had it and it was alive; pulsing, pushing and pulling. Its darkness had rubbed off on me back then, when I worked on the doors of the club for him, and it rubbed off on me again. I fed off of it as did the city from me. The city felt my return. I'd reached out when I returned to his bar. By stepping into it in the light of day it was like digging up and opening an unexploded bomb. I knew it, but went ahead and pulled the pin. I'd cut the cable and did it anyway. It was another reason to be there—the other for the boy.

SINCLAIR'S OYSTER BAR and the Wellington Inn forming Shambles Square had stood since the 1500s. It had survived The Arndale Shopping Centre being built around it in the 1970s and had survived the IRA's remodelling of the city centre. They'd used a 1500kg bomb, in '96. By 1999 the council saw fit to uproot it and replant the old boozer beam by beam. Satisfying the whim of the latest town planning idea.

I entered and noticed the prices hadn't changed much albeit the ceiling height had. Its previous level accounted for the average height of a drunkard in Tudor times. In 90s Manchester it needed an extra inch or two, and now it had it. It had saved me the bump on the head I used to get previously when crossing the threshold, or climbing the stairs to the bogs.

I ordered something to tie me over whilst sitting in the darkness of a back corner, away from the windows. I went through the case file again. I shifted my attention to Nancy's boy and his fall from the tower block in Salford. It wasn't far away and I'd saved cash for a cab. I needed to study up, refocus, and get myself there. I'd settle into the job the police had for me on the reception of the same building, and investigate. It'd be a base... a hideaway. It'd be nondescript enough to disappear into the grey background of the adjoining city of Salford. Almost as good as the witness protection in Bristol. I'd assimilate the tower block, its people, their flow. I'd look to understand and fix Nancy's ill feelings for the police and their statement to her—the message she'd been force-fed in the death of her boy: suicide.

She wasn't swallowing it.

Opening the file, it hit me that the police weren't giving away the whole story. It'd been changed. They'd held facts back. The picture forming was made intentionally incomplete. The main thing that just didn't look quite right to me. The supposed suicide note:

Mam, believe me – I've put in the effort.
I've done all that I can.
I'm embarrassed at the stuff I've been put through and
put you through.
And I'm ashamed of who I am:
A walking abortion.

It was a cut and paste job either by the police or the boy. Any fool without a helmet and badge could tell you where it had come from. Anyone with a Manc-pulse that is. I knew it was a mash-up of a band's lyrics, by the singer who's now dead from their very own suicide. The band went on under a new name: Altered-State and they were entwined with the club I used to work for. I used to guard the door of that club. Not that they'd know, as it was really owned and run by the villains, thugs, dealers and all them in-turn reporting into Mr Big. My predicament had grown and with it heightened senses. I took to looking over the top of the papers and re-reading them, scouting out who and what else was in there. These same senses would mean I'd spend the next few days increasingly watching my back; watching who I spoke to. I would play it all to my best advantage, to survive, get buy, get answers and get the fuck out when the jobs were done.

The lights flickered as evening drew in and as if the city itself was looking over my own shoulders. Nancy, the boy's mother, didn't buy the suicide note and neither did I. Looking at the note closely, it seemed to be the faded copy of a copy of a copy—grainy as hell. Maybe the police had taken her for a mug and had planted it to lead her into believing things were more palette-able than the truth. They'd steered her to believe he went down on his own accord. Or, maybe the boy had the lyrics lying about his flat and the police naively took it to be his own words. And from his mind at the time.

The author of the lyrics killed himself alright, but it wasn't the boy's—I knew it and so did his mother.

Something else stood out. Out of place, weird and wrong. There was a photo of the boy, or what was left, under a white sheet. Claret stained sheets; dark blood, almost black. The kind that leaves a body, soaking and fusing with whatever fabric it touches. It had formed a giant scab. His outline looked standard; a body, male, average height. But something odd bulged halfway down his body; poking at the stained white sheet like a gun, or a stick—up and straight out. It looked like he had a massive hard-on. A damn erection, sure as life, stood proud like the Blackpool tower. I didn't want to think about it anymore. But, it did look that way and I hoped his mother hadn't seen that particular photo. The invented path to believe, left by the police, made more sense now—for the sake of his mother. The boy's lost dignity, left shamed into the tarmac.

In the photo, even with the boy's apparent dead wood, the mass of people in the photo stood around, some police, some students, residents and onlookers all looking straight-faced. All were shocked and shaken out of whatever they were doing at the time when the boy passed their windows. A crack of flesh, bone and skull had rung out between the two tower blocks. There's not a smile in the crowd. All shaken by one of life's wakeup calls.

One girl, in her pyjamas, stared out of the picture at me. She glared out past me and into infinity and depth of time that opens up when life throws you into darkness like this. It shakes you awake enough to appreciate what you've got, for a while. But, beforehand it dulls you with an almighty shock and awe that can stop time itself. Life goes fast; take it for granted and it can slow right down; stop altogether. It reminds us on occasions like this and often it's all too late.

I took a drink and looked closer at the girl. She had stains around her mouth and chest; she'd touched the body... I looked into the notes again and saw her witness statement:

'I didn't know what to do; I tried mouth to mouth... It was too late. I tasted it: death. I didn't know what to do... I... I... tasted it... his death. We were meant to be going away together. The peaks—a walk in the hills—clear our heads. To get away from it for a bit. To take a break from this place. It was getting to us. It gets to everyone. Eventually. The taste... will it ever go?'

Carrie: Student. Aged 20. A resident of John L. Court.

YOU CAN'T BLOW life back into just anything. Not when it isn't there. And not when it isn't wanting it. The boy couldn't breathe. There wasn't enough left of him to take air into the lungs. It would seem all remaining life force had been redirected to his cock; to hold the sheet up like a big top tent. Life's priorities can be re-balanced in death it seems, though more extreme; honest maybe. The police statement didn't speculate if he was initially found in that state, whether it was post mortem or if she'd pumped him up to be found like that.

I looked at my drained glass and then back out of the window. I decided the drink and city was tainting my thinking; making it darker than it needed to be. Something in me had conjured up the dark images, and the case had it written all over; between the lines.

I needed to report in to my new vocation, on the tower block. And I needed to get to investigating at ground level, and to stop speculating sick imagined possibilities with the limits of this police folder and in the mother's own notes. Her's were a collection of emotive, vehement finger pointing back at the police. Whereas the police's were objective sounding side steps, misinformation and confident-sounding assumptions. All this mixed with absolute pure-shit. Neither was going to help.

I left to catch a black cab to the flats. People barged past me in the darkness as lights from the cars passed by shining intermittently in my eyes. I tasted it, like the girl in the photo had…the boy's death.

My taxi cut through the black rain as I thought about Cherry and our parting of ways on the train platform.

I wished we'd had a last kiss.

6

How Soon Is Now?

TWO GIANT MONOLITHIC tower blocks loomed up and over the taxi. One of which was to be my new base and home. Moonlit shadows reached out, dragging the car and me towards them. A high wire fence surrounded both; keeping the animals inside and out.

There they stood; two mass halls of residence blocks of teenagers and twenty-somethings, pre-loaded sacrificial lambs sent off by parents eager to get them out of the house. All had new bank cards, loans, computers and TVs. The blocks, inhabited by these students, were easy pickings for those in the poor surrounding council estates. Both buildings were fourteen storeys of 'pick and mix' treats to anyone dead-set on getting in, on robbing the inhabitants… or to throw themselves off the top to an unflinching ground below.

The security looked lax as I opened the double doors to reception. Then I realised that lax security—it was now me. A fat and sleepy-looking old woman, wearing a tabard, immediately entered from the double doors opposite me in the small lobby. She tossed me a bunch of keys then pointed to the glazed post office looking counter that had a window to the side of the lobby—a window to my new home. Footprints marked the wall below this window where visitors, residents and delivery staff had all leant on its small shelf, kicking away as they idled impatiently for answers from the other side of the glass that wouldn't come. And so, I'd hold-up myself on the other side. I'd wait for my own answers to come. Other stains higher up the wall, directly under the shelf looked like snot and trails of wet clothing and chipped paint from fidgeting fingernails. The cleaner left; no eye contact, nothing. I didn't think she'd be in on anything, part of the events or an undercover sent to watch over me. It had happened before. I was wary. You can tell when someone's carrying more than they're showing. Her basket was empty and she wanted out without a care for what was in mine...she was nothing in this. She was off to the bingo. I looked at the keys and picked out the only brass coloured Yale lock key, corresponding to the lock colour and opened the door adjacent to the window. The window that would be my eyes out.

The door eased open revealing a small box of a room, a desk below the lobby entrance window at the other side, and another window aiming to the car park and the other tower block opposite. Other than that there was only space for a small two-seater sofa, the stains of which I would reserve judgment on. Its staining was as obvious to me as the wall's but not as comfortable to contemplate. If I'd thought too hard it would result in me not using what would be my bed, settee and busted-up companion for a week or two. There was a mini-fridge to the side of the sofa and I looked in it expectantly. It was empty but for what I hoped was a small bit of cheese—I wasn't sure. At the back, door-less hinges hung alone, with no door in the frame through to a tiny windowless room with a shower cubicle, sink and toilet bowl. I pulled the light cord inside and the tired yellow-stained fluorescent tube overhead clicked and flickered on revealing fully occupied fly strips and the whole state left to me.

I noticed the present left to me in the toilet bowl and looked into the speckled rusty mirror alongside. It was dotted from the tired black paint to the reverse, and from an assault of bored blackhead squeezing by those before me. It was hard for me not to feel sorry for the person who'd been caged up in here before me. Their residue inevitably led to hatred when I had to touch items and move around the space. This went on… with the tap handle which spluttered, coughing up air, rust and mud before gifting me the water I'd asked for.

It was all bad but I'd stayed in worse, with and without the facility of it all. Only the poor, those wanting, at war, with pain and without anything knew that feeling. And to find gratitude in a box like this. Rather than underground.

I splashed water on my face and laid on the sofa and my legs dangled over the end.

Crossing my arms and closing my eyes I attempted to count jumping sheep to send myself to sleep…

There's no sheep, they're all Cherry and there's no fence to jump either, just the dead boy under the white, blood-stained sheet that's pushed up with an erection from underneath.

I sleep like a log; like a dead man. No one jumps over me.

And I don't have wood.

MONDAY, AT 7.30AM: 'Wake up,' a male voice barely audible touched me in my sleep, sounding like a whisper from another time and place. 'Wake up' again it whispered, slightly louder. 'WAKE UP FUCKER!' Words shouted again, hitting me like a door blown shut in the wind, or a hand slammed on a table. I snapped to, falling from the two-seater onto the floor, bringing with me a stained cushion that toppled to the floor with the same lack of grace as me. It revealed the guts of the sorry sofa, springs pushing bare fabric, a half biscuit and a pocket full of forgotten coins.

I looked up from my kneeling position to see a postman at the lobby window. I also saw curtains on a rail which I could have pulled closed the night before; saving me some face. Goodness knows how many residents had already left to go to work seeing my carcass snoring, rolling and farting away through the lobby window.

'That folds out into a bed you know?'

'No, I didn't,' I croaked with my throat feeling the cigarettes and alcohol. I must have looked the part even if I was late for the first delivery of the day.

'This pile of shit's for you, this building and these twats – Sign here,' and he dumped a pile on the shelf the other side of the glass; shoving a sheet through the slot under the window and a chewed up Biro pen. I staggered forward, and with each step I transformed. By the third step, I'd regained my mind and body and he saw I was no security guard. My eyes alone cut through the glass-like black bullets. His ego shrank and I didn't think he'd sound off again even with the door and glass partition between us. I signed his sheet and he left to go back to his rounds and the safety of his post office rounds. A world safe from the danger of mine; drinking, writing, solving life—one bastard at a time.

The keys I'd got the night before included the brass Yale lock key which let me into the shit hole lobby flat. Another, I guessed, was the lobby doors and a master key. And there were ones for the communal doors and a master for the individual flats themselves. I considered checking the register, for regular deliveries or with my absent employers to see if one of the flats were vacant so I could take over it for a while instead of holding up in that hole, then I dismissed it. The lobby bedsit had a good vantage point. I could see who was in the block, their visitors, monitor overall comings and goings and what was going on. I could get a feel for who knew what and what went on that night, with the kid.

SALFORD'S SHOPPING CENTRE took a few sorry minutes to walk to. Pendleton district's finest. It was hard not to imagine being trapped inside a slasher film or computer game when I arrived. Kappa tracksuit wearing Zombies leered from aisles, doorways, from behind prams, pushchairs and mobility scooters. Sports Direct must have had an unwritten contract with the council as well as Benson & Hedges. I grabbed a pre-packed breakfast sandwich, some bottles of both hard and soft liquids and headed back. I realised I was blending in more than I cared to contemplate and for reasons that were not all bad, with the ultimate end result: camouflage.

I pulled up a chair behind the glass window of my cage, opened the bottles and ate my fuel for the day. Taking out the black and red notebook, I released the elastic binding and it started over again and I wrote on.

THE BLOCK OCCUPANTS came, they passed, they ignored and they sneered. I gave up the idea, letting it pass, of masturbating under the desk—for fear of a splinter. I looked under the top and saw one or two staples hanging out that would have caught me like a fish hook and I was glad I hadn't tempted fate. I re-examined the police file and I went over it again, making more notes:

Made up suicide note?
By the Police? By the boy? Why?

Just a lyric sheet from a band found in his room? Or, put there?
What truth is there to hide?
What's hidden in his 'sexed-up' death?
Is that secret enough to cover over, for Mother? YES.
Seedy, sex, death—dead boy's pole up?

The lines of questions stopped me then I looked at the keys again…and wrote:

The boy—a resident here, or was he just visiting?

I went back to the file: he used to be in one of the University College Salford flat units; made up of three small rooms in what should have been one complete flat in its own right: 10th floor, 7th flat, room C.

I looked at the keys again, and the potential master key. I decided to wait till dark, let myself in and get a feel for the space, the memories and his state of mind. I felt a resonance; the boy, the block, the people, and the ground it all stood on; darkness even in the light of day. A lot of Salford and Manchester could feel like that anyway. Like a Lowry painting shown on a black and white TV with bad reception, but I saw and felt past that.

There was something else here—something a lot worse.

Resting my head on the desktop below the window to the lobby, I closed my eyes for a dose; recharging for the work ahead.

I woke up.

A tall, dark-haired, smug man said: 'I really love that shirt!' waking me before I'd had a chance to rest up. It looked like he was on his way out for the evening. He quipped his little gem of a condescending comment, then turned to this vacant looking blonde thing by his side. A cheeky grin, her approval, and a peck on his cheek from her was the reward he was after. I thought, then returned fire: 'Well done fucker… Loving it?'

I asked, sitting up slightly with my black-eye-bullets tightening straight at him.

'Yeah, I'm really loving it,' he said, sniggering again and turned back to her. It's senseless, and they must have seen my dissonance with them. And with it a danger. Maybe they didn't though. They must have been stoned. This must have been a regular ritual for them. As much as putting on their favourite album to get them in the mood before going out. And as much as a quick fast-fuck before leaving; emptying any of his potential temptations from the rest of the dance floors they pranced over for the night.

I decided to play the game further and toy with their jibes: 'Is that the love between a man and a woman, or a man and a man?' I glared through the glass checking out his girlfriend, trying to provoke something back.

'A platonic love, my shitty little friend, a platonic love!' he returned, attempting to shut me down. I'd upset his flow and his routine. He knew I wasn't the usual caged monkey waiting to be prodded in here; trapped in this tiny glazed underclass shell, waiting for his target practice—the prick.

'Ah, a platonic love. That's what you say. Is that like the love between a young boy and his trusty old pet donkey then? Aww— living by the sea together?' I feigned a look of understanding and then another of dumb blank innocence. My eyes meanwhile stirred up a hell and he knew it. I tried to be light-hearted but I was carrying too much suffering for this light-hearted bull-shit-banter. My eyes gave it away and scared the man, however, she was just oblivious, stoned and on another planet altogether.

'Yes, platonic, just like that,' he said nervously but still smug enough for me to return further fire. He returned a look at his girl for more approval; checking that she was still on side; that she was paying attention and unaffected by my game change that cornered him.

'But what if the donkey eats some seaweed?' I spat out at them through gritted teeth.

He quivered at me: 'W-w-what?'

'Some stinking FUCKING seaweed,' and the words left my still gritted teeth carried on a simmering rage. 'With some shellfish or crab in it maybe?' I asked, but didn't want an answer. Now she shifted her adoring gaze; moving it from his designer stubbled jawline and had become aware of the temperature change; the shift in control in the small claustrophobic reception lobby. She sensed this and stepped tentatively towards the doors, pulling at his hand, to suggest they leave.

'What?' he said, almost in a trance, fixed to the spot.

'Yes, the donkey eats some seaweed. There's some shellfish in there. The shellfish does what shellfish does—An aphrodisiac. That little boy's in for a world of hurt!'

'Let's go... NOW!' she said quivering and tugging at his arm eagerly.

'Now,' I said, 'Fuck off' and I reached for a half-finished bottle of beer, took a swig then I continued: 'so, how much do you really like this shirt? Donkey fucker. As much as a boy-shagging mule? Have–a–good–night.'

He looked confused, dazed and all that's in between. She just looked scared and relieved it was just words between us.

'Goodnight' I said to the doors as they closed behind them. I picked up my notebook, the keys and put on my jacket.

The boy's flat called out to me through the floors above. It was time.

7

Interzone

METAL DOORS SHUDDERED and slid open revealing a stained, dimpled-metallic-skin. The once reflective mirrored surface above the handrail was a mass of stickers, and dried on phlegm and cum. The whole lift stank of the piss, dead souls and worse that lingered there.

A lone light flickered and I walked in as the entire box rocked. Just enough to remind me I was suspended by unseen wires. And that was probably just as tired as the dank shell I stood in. I'd be hanging from the rusty frayed cords all the way to the tenth. It taunted, shuddering again as the doors shut... and again starting its tired accent.

Blackout:

The lights cut out, holding for an extended time, then flashed on long enough for me to see a vision: the boy in there with me. He looked down through the metal box's floor to the ground below us that would take him. After he went all the way to the top floor, broke through the service hatch on the roof and went over the edge.

A flicker of the lights again... I saw Cherry standing there. She looked as if we'd said all we could. And all we should... before we parted on the platform. She moved in to kiss me; to give us the last kiss we never had. A real kiss to share it all, showing more than the lust, sex and filler we'd had up until then. I could feel her breath as her lips moved nearer to mine and parted. I could see moisture to her bottom lip as we eagerly awaited contact.

A flash again. And it was Mr. Big—in place of Cherry. His shaven, bulky, scarred head and face was a hair's breadth from mine. He drooled. Revelled. And whispered through gritted teeth: 'Kiss this cop-cunt would ya? Ya stinking pig fucker!!' snarling the threat through spit and bile… then he disappeared. He faded into the background.

With another strobe of the light, my Viking, the ghost of my heritage and my strength and counterpart was there opposite me. He silently fed my spirit with iron. He stared a history's worth of grit into me. Then he disappeared.

We all came to an abrupt shuddering halt in the capsule of my torment.

THE DOORS STARTED to open, struggling. A flood of faded fluorescents filled the box I was in. I looked down in a mini-trance. A meditation for what was ahead. I closed my eyes then stepped forward into the corridor, and into the case, getting nearer and nearer to the boy's flat and what lay waiting for me. I didn't pass another soul. Chewing gum and fag burns clagged the carpet underfoot. The walls by the lift were a messed-up canvas where people had been waiting, scribbling, picking and scratching in some kind of idle madness. I walked the corridor, reading the occasional in-joke comments, insults and riddles that were pencilled on the walls at intervals the width of each flat's demise. Some seemed like aimless banter and some carried another story and a point. I made a note of some of them as I walked to Flat 7 at the end of the corridor:

'Farmyard loves Moles' xxx'

'Call Gary for Gange or Flange—anytime!' 'Skank Bladder—Pour

Homme. Base notes of
Boddingtons, scotch and fox shit.'

And in a giant scrawl down a couple of meters of wall:

'Transference & Rebirth.'

Then a small note that had a scrawled symbol next to it of a combined exclamation mark and question mark...maybe it was an 'S' overlapping an 'I' or a snake and sword... maybe both—the author wasn't much of an artist. Then they'd written underneath:

'If you think Burroughs was right. Follow the red light to the Cities of the Red Night.'

I reached the front of the boy's flat. The police tape over the front masked a number 7. My eyes moved to the ceiling tiles. The one over the front door had been turned over, moved slightly. Lots of them are like that in the building, this one bothered me... I pulled up a sorry looking blue padded chair next to the nearby fire extinguisher and stood on it. And reached up and flipped the tile. That symbol was there again. Drawn in red marker on the reverse. The symbol of the overlapping S and I that was next to the Transference & Rebirth scrawl I'd seen. The note that was also near the Burroughs' reference to Cities of the Red Night and to follow a red light, if you thought he was right. Scratching at the surface; connections were forming. I lit a pre-rolled cigarette, taking a self-congratulatory lung full. The irony of the slow smoker's suicide versus the boy's quick jump wasn't lost on me. I turned the tile back over and threw myself from the chair to get on with his death riddle.

I ripped at the police tape; left it hanging to the frame. Lucky with the first key I tried on the fob, it was the master key—it turned. The lock's click echoed its sinister point.

Dank musty mist filled the flat corridor. This had an empty despair different from my residence. I saw three doors with letters ahead: A and B were immediately in front of me and C was at the end of the corridor on the right with more police tape over it. Another two doors were on the same side: a bathroom and a kitchen.

I continued to smoke, exhaling and adding to the misty, stale atmosphere. I was glad as my nicotine won over, overpowering the resident smell emanating from the residue of a once busy, tightly packed, sweaty and steamy place. No windows had been left open, the Venetian blinds were down. The only light came from the open door I'd come through and the tip of my smoke. I heard voices in the main corridor behind and quickly shut the front door. Shutting myself in. I tried the light switch next to me… it didn't work. The power, water and anything else must have been shut off. Together with the police tape, the lack of power kept the chance of a squatter and any new residents out. Only ghosts and an atmosphere remained; a tainted aura of loss.

I walked slowly towards the door at the end: 'C'. A helicopter hovered outside, likely scouting for the latest Strangeways escapee on the run from the police. A searchlight streamed in through the kitchen window blinds, like a laser, cutting linear shadows through my smoke and across all the floor and walls. Dust and small flies seemed to hover in its stream. As it passed, the dust seemed to move up towards the ceiling. Then, it was dark again, leaving just me, the ghosts, smoke, dust and a fear of the outside world. The searchlights from the helicopter magnified a growing anticipation. My heart pounded as I controlled my breathing.

In the kitchen, I ran the tap over my cigarette and pushed it into the plughole. I parted the blinds enough to see out and saw the helicopter's silhouette against the city skyline. A light beam was fixed firmly on the footbridge over the dual carriageway outside. I squinted but there was nothing to make out. Maybe another jumper, this time from a different spot. I supposed, from the footbridge, if the fall didn't get them a passing taxi or truck would. Suicide is more common than people realise. It's only when you're touched by it personally that you acknowledge the growing numbers and the statistics, previously ignored, on page four or five of the daily rag. If only people could see the growing pile of bodies on the front with a footballer's latest failed conscience... or on page three with their own.

I took out my notebook; the words I used covered the ambience with suggestions and suppositions. A resonance leftover from the boy. Then, I headed to the main event; the door to his room.

Unlocked, I walked straight in; surprised at this lack of effort needed or any resistance by life. I opened it up fully and saw why it was all so fucking easy. The room had been stripped, nothing was there. Even the carpet has been lifted leaving the sorry stained concrete; stains of spills, thrills and bellyaches, but no blood. The searchlight started waving around again, cutting through the room. My silhouette span about the room like a pissed sundial. The door closed slowly behind me on a mechanism and I heard faint muffled loudspeaker of shouts from outside:

'Come down from there,' then a pause as they addressed onlookers, 'nothing to see here. Close your windows. NOW!'

I turned slowly following the path of the searchlight as it arced up the flats. Passing inside it lit up the back of the door. A trace of something reflected in the light. Something that'd recently been washed off. A pen that was used, paint or pencil residue remained behind. Although cleaned off, it had left a film glinting in the light. In parts there was a slight indentation as if someone had pressed to write on the door. I saw it: that logo again. The S and I artwork worked into a question mark mixed with exclamation mark motif. It was the same as on the tile outside the front door, but with an extra mark at the bottom. The light passed over and past the door, making everything invisible again. I knelt down and stared at the door and took out my matt black Zippo and flicked it on. Its flame wasn't intense enough though and I couldn't quite see. The helicopter helped out again, with another pass. And the stream started to go over the room again anticlockwise. I stared waiting for a glimpse at what the last mark was. Slowly the beam shifted around the room, stuttering as if it might change direction at any moment, then it gave me what I wanted. It lit the door up in front of my face, reflecting in the markings below the logo and there it was right in front of my face. My heart stopped as I read it:

[S.I.- 696]

The club I used to work for numbered everything. They catalogued every finite detail with the owners; the record company. More an artistic expression in branding than an exercise in organisation itself. It was an organised chaos at best from their side which was why the gangs took over and exploited it; so in-turn became the real bosses in control. Their numbering was on band albums and singles covers, people, places and events. This code to the boy's door was more than a toy with the number of the beast. It suggested a connection of the boy to my other troubles. Seeing this mark, made me feel sick. There was no reason not to think someone hadn't borrowed the numbering protocol. The link was unsettling to my core. I was there to settle that score; the links to the Mr. Big of gangland Manchester. I resented the apparent overlapping interest with my other case. Now, they were becoming one. It was sure to make me less under the radar as I started to sniff around. I was hoping to confront those demons as extra-curricular activities—safely outside of the boy's case.

Manchester and Salford are big physically and carry a psychological weight too. They share canals, bloodlines, rivers, clubs, roads and gangsters. Of course it was all to be linked. Confirmation bias or not. This became the case and my reality. The sickness passed, I stood slowly and embraced this new twist in the tail of what might be all the same job. I sketched the logo motif and the number. It was an auto-response, reflex—how could I forget.

I left, hurried along by a scream from the corridor.

Opposite the flat entrance, a Geordie girl screeched to her girlfriend as they looked out of the window: 'They chopped his fookin' heed off. Mental pet. Sheer mental.'

I approached them cautiously from behind. The view wasn't much.

'Sorry?' I said. The words and my presence didn't cause a turn. They were held transfixed by the events that unfolded on the bridge outside.

They replied eventually without a care who I was: 'Aye, head off… chop,' and one of them made a chopping motion on the window ledge with their hand, 'fucking Triads, in- it… Chinkies.'

'Stop it Shaz, my stomach thinks me throat's bin cut n' all—could eat a chinky right now.'

'Ooh aye, chips n' curry sauce.' the other joined. Minds

already shifted from the horror show below.

'People forget Chinatown's there. Until they steal the wrong car or spill the wrong drink,' I interrupt.

'They won't forget this time…fuck me…head's clean off man… head… OFF! Choppy-chop-chop!' one exclaims.

'Stop talking aboot fookin' food pet—seriously' the other went.

'Didn't roll very far though did it?!' The other said.

'Ooh sausage roll…' I heard one mutter, then left them. I could hear laughs as the door to the stairwell clunked behind.

They'll forget alright, Chinatown that is. They always do, until someone stupid sticks a pin in it all again, a stick or a bullet and then it steps back out. The sleeping dragon goes through those decorated gates, into the rest of the city. It would take 'till the next time for the city to forget again. And wish it hadn't woken that beast again. Even the gangs of Moss Side treated it like a foreign no-go camp complete with invisible high walls and locked gate…until curry night:

'Table for four gangsters from Longsight is it? Right you are sirs. You'll be having unbeknown cat-head-soup or dog's-ass-Manchuian then… Happy with that? Or is it a chef's special you're after?: Informant's severed head Szechwan. Or, special offer today: the sweet and sour cops' balls?'

I regretted taking the stairs after the third flight down. By the tenth my legs burned—I was ready to puke. By the bottom step, I did puke. I left for The Woolpack, next door. I needed another eye-opener and something to wash the taste away.

I passed through the rows of retired gangster's Jags and Range Rovers parked outside and looked if any plates rang a bell. None did.

Ding ding. It was round two. In every sense.

8

Driftwood

A mass of fat backs teetered on sorry bar stools. Body masses, lumps that could be whales or Orcas, bobbed along in the smog of the place. The thick smoke settled halfway up the old bar. They continued their idle nodding, farting and occasional gaze to an infinity of shame residing in the bar's mirror. Eyes were firmly fixed. My presence only slightly lifted them. As they adjusted temporarily from the crosswords and ashtrays they were filling.

I ordered and took a drink. A stained built-in bench in the corner was all there was left. No familiar threats hid there that I could see. All just driftwood floating harmlessly underwater, breaking apart one whiskey at a time. And, a travesty representation of the criminal underworld; all whose time had passed. The Jags on the curbs outside were just remnants of egos that once meant something. Now there was a harsh new breed ruling the streets and clubs. I'd been there, worked it and seen it close up front. They'd probably felt it as I entered. Maybe the new breed occasionally popped in there to pull rank on yesterday's gangsters. They didn't care... they had done their time. In and out, now glad to enjoy a nip above ground. And in front of the right kind of bars, free of Strangeways.

The drink touched the sides of my sobriety and like the fat lumps by the bar, pushed me over. But, unlike them, it also lit a fuse rather than dousing it out. I took a sip to counter an ill effect from the hangover and the unwilling exercise earlier. Then, took another mouthful and moved on. Towards action. One way or another I would have a bad head in the morning. If the beer didn't give it, this dark-city would. I was about to reach out, stick a pin in it myself. Not Chinatown though.

I went to leave. I decided to ask a few questions first; about the boy. I approached the bar, notebook in hand. Both were for show, effect, and an invisible threat of authority that I was going to write whether they talked or not.

'Just one last thing...' I borrowed a line from a TV detective. With it came the suggestion I knew something already. Also, the interaction with them before-hand, that never was. A historical act I remembered... and they'd forgotten. As it was, there was absolute zilch. Not a thing between us all in there then... or ever. They were smoked-out ghosts on Death's door. Or already inside and I was the unwanted visitor from the other side.

The barman, a gaunt washed-out statue of a man, stared through me. He looked like he'd been part of the place since day one; a retired old-school gangster of yesterday. There was a bleached out old Polaroid behind the bar of him, with a rifle leant up against him as a younger self. If you blinked it was the archetypal Lee Harvey Oswald shot. If you looked longer it was a cocky young criminal playing Billy-Big-Balls just like the rest. It didn't impress, I'd seen a different era of criminal in this city, and about as up-close and personal as anyone would dare, before getting the fuck out. These old bastards didn't stand a chance out there these days and they knew it.

'The boy?' I said. The barman wasn't going to talk first so I did and mimicked his stare right back at him.

'Boy?' he rasped. I'm not sure how used to conversing he was in there. I was glad he was starting to open up a bit. It felt like it was going to be a long, dead interview. I took out a pen and opened the notebook, letting the red elastic snap, again for the sheer drama of it all.

'The dead boy?'

'Togs did it,' he said as a matter of fact. It assured my instant interest. I was expecting to draw blood from a stone, suck it out till my lips hurt. Or, I just gave up. Out it came again and more: 'Togs did it... I told the last one and now I'm telling you it. When are people going to stop regurgitating this shit to make money out of the dead lad...? You aren't a copper, you're a fucking hack or writer... they're all at it. Leave him rest, let him be... he gave the city enough.' he ranted on. His rehearsed act had been done before, that was clear, even if his rambled outburst wasn't so much.

'I'm investigating for her: his Mam.'

'His Mam. Is she even still alive? Told you Togs fucking did it. Look at anyone standing to gain from a death and chances are it is them. Surprised the fucking pigs haven't figured it out yet... Mind, he probably paid them off. With the cost of that first still pic he sold to the magazines.'

'Togs? A still?'

'Pho-tog-rapher. And, a still photograph,' he clarified as if talking to a first-time hack; unused to the lingo. 'The photographer did it and now he's made for life with a few snaps; making 'em black and white, choosing the dark ones. Touting pictures of a ghost that was never there. They're building up this icon most of the world hadn't heard of. Now they all want the fucking t-shirt. None of them heard the sodding music—fuck sake. Now he's god. And we'd all like a piece of that wouldn't we?!' his words reached some sort of finishing crescendo.

I realised yet again, another story had more resonance than the one I was actually there to ask about.

My case, the boy, had thrown himself from one of the tower blocks next door to their local boozer. They would have heard his head bounce from their barstools. But, they were oblivious at the time. It'd meant nothing to them. But… the lead singer from a band, killed himself decades ago, and it's like we all built a mountain high statue over the city.

Its shadow never shifts.

'That's shit. Interesting, but pure fucking dog-shit!' I said delivering the perfect inverted shit sandwich and an iced-over stare. No pretence. 'Surely by that thinking, the fucking record label could have done it too—they've never sold so many. Or the fucking Universities, no one gave a shit about coming here until the music meant something outside of the city walls… or…what about the FUCKING club. It needed the press more than anything. It was packed every night; haemorrhaging cash left right and centre.' The words pained me to say it as I'd worked for the place, seen its corruption. No part of me actually believed it could have been involved. Truth of the matter is we are all involved; everything, and everyone. We were symptoms; casualties of a hedonistic fuelled epoch. But in the end, he was a victim only to himself. And now it's a fucking poster. And… it's an unprinted and unsaid uni' and college prospectus. Drawing student youth and new blood to be spilt to the city.

I corrected my course of inquiry in my head and remembered the two strong cases I was on. The one for me and one for the other boy. There was no escaping the gravity of either anywhere for me, not for a hundred miles.

'I'm actually referring to the boy that hit the tarmac, not thirty feet from this bar I was leant on a moment ago—your fuckin' bar. He died and the police covered it in some lame story and the mother wants to know the what, the why, and how. His name was William B. Rowes… Maybe remember for next time?'

I closed my book and went to leave. The elastic snapped hard. The barman's was another broken record in a town full of them. His words spoke of a different dead soul, the one who wrote the lyrics that were found in the boy's flat. The ones confused for a suicide note. My boy and case, it would seem, were already forgotten or never known in the first place. As most of the city was concerned, there was only one suicide. The one that made a god—the one that put it on the map; gave birth to another band, its extended recognition and so killed its ability to go on without a new order to things. Again everything was entwined in the bitter fabric of the place—deep roots to a bare tree.

I began to hear voices again. I guessed at least one of them wasn't in my head. Some old bastard of a gangster nearly fell over trying to get off his stool to talk to me. As I opened the door to leave, he waved something in his hand; a flyer to give me.

'A little help son,' he said. A lifetime of drinking, smoking and worse was carried in the words to me in an air heavy with their past pains. I took and opened it. It was a club night logo again, similar to the S.I. one I'd found in the block of flats. Clearly, by the same artist; there was an address and time:

'Launderette'—Bands / DJ Indie night The BOARDWALK
Whitworth Street
8pm 'till whenever-am

'It's a sad day when used-to-be's are helping out could-of-beens,' I said submissively. Actually grateful.

'Don't be so hard on yourself son. Some people respect what you did… Would like *him* gone too,' he said, referring to my own case. I got who they referred to. Mr. Big wasn't generally liked.

A name on the mast-head of the ship no one wanted to be on. Because, they knew where it was going.

'Thanks' I said, meeting him in the middle and growing more on his side.

'Now fuck off out our pub!' he snarled. I saw an old demon of yesteryear in his eyes.

So, I fucked off. If I was still standing in 30 odd years maybe there'd be a place at the bar for me—not now.

As one door opened in front, another shut behind. That pub wasn't only just a line of inquiry, it was more a lining of the stomach and a bracer. I pushed on.

It's only when you're well again, you truly appreciate how sick you were. And when you're found, that's when you discover how lost you were.

I was sick but on track, with both destinations to solve; the boys drop to the ground and my own issues with the clubland cesspool; the one I thought I'd cured in court. Mr. Big had clearly bounced the court, and I was going for him. I could smell him all over the boy's case too, that and whatever shithouse club he was held up in. It could be The Boardwalk; that explained why the gangland coffin dodgers had pointed me there.

9

A Rush and a Push and the Land is Ours

A LONE DOVE sat on a road sign. It cooed as I passed over the virtual line from one city to another. The sign read: 'You are leaving Salford, Welcome to Manchester!'.

'FUCK RIGHT OFF!' was underneath in manic red paint. Not aimed at anyone in particular, it was a vented spleen from a lost soul looking to be heard—from a place full of them.

Salford and Manchester are fused together with veins of canals and waterways. Regardless, it still felt like a lifetime to walk the A6 and cross the border between them.

Alongside me emerged an ever-changing collage of wall posters, band promos and club night flyers. Like peeling skin; denser and denser rich layers formed a tapestry of faded epochs in time. One seemed to weep last night's rain back out at me. The pavements texture, a matter of the ages, and those walls made for rich treacle-like consistency to pass through. I pushed against it and ground my feet into the pavement. I recognised one band's name and it conjured up memories of the club I'd worked at:

They'd played there… And had gone by a few names: The Fakes, Montebacks and then the Imposters or some other Charlatan-type stamp. The atmosphere of the club was split in two on my favourite nights—I preferred the live bands. And they would often be pushed into a small blacked out back room. It was a room of sweaty moshers. Whereas the main cathedral-like space was a separate zoo-like mass of pill heads with a DJ working them into a frenzy from a booth high above.

From memory, that band was doing ok on the night. In the intimacy of the smaller room.

They'd played out of their heads most times during their peak. During their troughs too. Once, I caught the keyboard player mid-song as he leant back and fell off the stage. He'd been so far gone he'd forgotten which way the audience was, and was sat with his back teetering on the stage edge. In one euphoric hammering of the keys, he went over and I caught him. I pushed him back and he played on—he didn't miss a single note—talented fuck.

Things had moved on… The bassist was doing time. The drummer: gone AWOL. And the rest, disappeared into the depths of semi-mainstream success; leaving the darkness of Rain City for good. They surfed the hit-parade, safe from the place that had birthed their success—free to be whatever they liked.

WAFTS OF SULPHUR and egg emanated from the Brewery nearby as I walked towards Manchester. A distinct smell; a somewhat soapy beer: Boddingtons. The smell hung in the air like the city's own fart. With all our noses shoved firmly under the covers. There was no escape, we just had to learn to love and live with it.

Road signs to Strangeways (prison) pointed the way to old comrades, pals and enemies. I knew the best and worst were still on the streets ahead of me. Lighting the way to my journey's end.

It was all to evolve into a game of Russian roulette with myself. As I dipped in and out of the pubs, clubs and bars until I turned up as a bad penny—hoping for the one link that led to a jackpot: solving the boys fall. And felling Mr Big—that was gonna be a bonus.

He was close now… getting closer.

My suppository sized mobile phone went off: 'RING RING.' 'Written yet?' asked my agent, confidant and the she-devil on my shoulder.

'This shit writes itself—like last time. You know how it is for me.'

'Just checking up on you. Checking you're not just in a fuckin' pub—I do know what you're actually like J.'

'Fair enough—you back to stripping? This gonna be a long call, or got a punter's nuts in your lap… I know what you like too.'

'Listen…' she said, and 'breathe the old place in… Take your time… Breathe it out. It'll stick better that way. To you, them, the readers, and the page,' she added.

'The air is thick with it all. Still stinks—of my past. All that's coming too. I've dug it right up back up again.' I resigned out loud.

'You were born into this. Just make sure you finish it… d'ya know what I mean?'

'I know—thanks for the confidence boost M. As always—a foot up the arse.'

'Don't play sensitive, you're such a big boy,' she flirted, purring. And I felt a tingle as she toyed at my primal instincts. 'Shouldn't you get back to your punters? Seriously… Another pint to pour? Or are you getting them out again one
last time for the boys?'

'Cheeky, cheeky—CLICK,' and she was gone. I could see her wink as she did it, across the radio waves; saucy old cow.

I touched the notebook in my pocket. She had restored another focus in me. The fight was on. As was the recording and restoration of the self.

I HAD NEVER thought of myself as a writer or a Private Investigator. Turns out I was living it; from the first case—the one that made me. The one that introduced me to her; Mademoiselle Pampelmousse and the other woman; Cherry; my lost kiss from the station platform.

I couldn't escape it or the soldier inside—inescapable back then... on the doors too. The soldier, the SAS infantry and the street-soldier for hire by the thugs and gangs working the club doors. I couldn't shake free of any of it... Maybe this whole P.I. thing was the natural course of a river and my past was the tributaries feeding it... This new fight felt the right type of wrong. Previously, my battles for other people's politics and the drug lords of the city were all wrong.

THE CRYING WALLS of stone continued as I walked on. A short bald tattooed man appeared from a side street in front of me. He pulled at and yanked a small boy along behind: a son. Across the road outside a corner shop, a girl was rearranging some fruit and veg boxes. The boy laughed as his father gazed and drooled over her curves. The boy then got a surprise clip round the ear accompanied with viscerally barked words:

'I DON'T TOUCH PAKIS!'

I heard it clearly from my few yards away. My buried hackles and rage levels flew up; my temperature too. The father's words were like bricks thrown idly around a playground—ignorant and damaging.

My own prejudices dressed him down: In my head I saw his virtual white van, a copy of The Sport on the front dash, and in the back were tools for an idle trade. Ones that had been half-worked between the hours of eight and three each weekday. Then he has a pint or four before returning home to the estate where they lived. A sorry wife hides in the kitchen or backyard hanging washing. He'd claim rights over her... like those calluses on his palms somehow validated his actions. That wife that had settled for the love she thought she'd deserved back then. And so took his abuse. Because that's how people go on in their world. I heard their inner selves:

'We've always treated each other this way. Dad had, Mother had... And what's all this change, and what's all these foreign people around here now—it's all their fault; this change—that and the cold dinner you gave me—and the black eye I gave you back—and this child we had too young because you said 'no', but I took you anyway. And that child we fill up with our daily fucked-up hate machine of words, actions, inactions. Our children continue looking to us expecting the world and we give it to them; OUR WORLD: narrow-viewed, restricted, blinkered and racist... All this when they started off so open to life and love—full of opportunity. And who gives a FUCK. We'll give them no chances and no hope, so they can end up just like us... Make us proud!'

I knew it all too well. Their warts were my own. Past scars remained where I'd tried to rid myself of them. My years in service had washed away a few, but others ran deep. Managed and kept in check by an ever-growing tired conscience, topped. up with bad thoughts, cheap beer, wine and fags.

A further 25 yards down the pavement and the man leered again. Another girl bent over to tie her laces on the opposite side of the road. She was slender; wearing tight trousers. He saw an invitation to gawp where there wasn't one. Took advantage dominated her image and used her in his head.

'Muffler pants' he muttered to the boy, dragging him on—eyes fixed firmly on target.

'Muffler pants?' the boy puzzled; confused by the comment and his father's continued seedy letching.

'Yes, muffler pants son—look… you can see the lips moving but you can't hear what they're saying!' he grinned, so pleased with himself. He laughed and stared on, licking his lips. Then he turned mean; pissed off at the boy's continued confusion. 'You better not be a fookin' woofter boy! I'll drown you in the fuckin' canal right now.'

The bald meat-head extended his uninvited looks, piercing the girl's clothes; dirtying her body with his stare. He stole one last seedy shot for his minds-eye to use on himself later on; looking deep into her.

Then he walked forward… Straightened up…

And, cracked square into a lamp post.

The full force of his thick frame rattled the hard pole.

His nose cracked open against the old cast iron in a splatter of blood. It sprayed silhouetting the pole perfectly over the pavement—a work of art.

I winced, grinned myself now at the pure justice in his pain. All three of us looked at the bald man—the boy, me and the girl. A fire had been lit; a fuse was gonna go.

She'd stood upon hearing the clatter of metal, grizzle and bone. And as she finished standing up she revealed a pretty face… An Indian face. The child laughed harder, losing all control this time. He giggled, holding his mouth. Unable to hold it in, it escaped out the sides of his hands through sprays of spit and wriggling fingers.

The dad went to take his fist back and take the full force of his embarrassment, pain and fury out on the boy.

I caught him by the wrist.

His knuckles were left resting a mere inch from the boy's startled little freckled face. What is now a well-used look came from my blackened-over eyes—piercing his child-beating soul. A look that told of movements that could stop a heart. I felt like hitting him. Adding to what fate and the lamp post had already dished out.

Blood trickled from his face—shiny black rivers flowed from each flared nostril. His son was scared. And I didn't want to become the bad guy and so martyr the pig-head father.

The mark of the post would remain. I left the lesson to be learnt, released his wrist, without any real protest. He hadn't realised I'd been there all along, just behind him. Next time, maybe he'd feel me watching over.

By the second shake of his wrist, I floated on—gone.

If I'd started that fight, the one against the division, the social ignorance and meat-heads I knew I'd be distracted and stuck way too long in the myre. It'd take a decade or more to try to mend that; I wasn't enough.

AGAIN, I MOVED forwards on the road to nowhere, and everywhere. Chewing gum speckled tarmac and concrete as broken slabs became my anti-red carpet to welcome me in. The urban conveyor belt to hell—in resolution and revolution.

Band promos and posters for more recent bands gathered density and frequency alongside me. Most depicted moody looking characters with Beatles-esque hair, thick eyebrows and teeth that could only mean they hadn't broken America yet. They'd need some work for the superficial skin-deep masses across the Atlantic.

I ripped at the corner of one of the posters on the way past and carried the top half along with me. The name of the band looked like something familiar, a shoe shop, a shopping centre, an outlet selling clothes for middle-aged frumps... I dropped it. The image of the band had already burnt an image on the back of my retinas: slug-like eyebrows, thick mop-top hair and broken northern stares.

I stopped on Trinity footbridge over the River Irwell, linking both cities. Created from a fag-packet sketch from an architect's studio in Milan, it was one massive giant spike. Suspension wires held it taught, tethering it back, appearing to keep it from firing it off into outer space where it belonged.

More than both cities felt worth. The ostentatiousness of the bridge was lost. A soup of cans, sweaters, shopping trolleys and detritus flowed below, as the guts of both cities were shat from the many waterways that fed it. The bridge's statement may have been lost but the audacity rang true in both cities' people.

Folk went missing all the time in those watery polluted veins. Always had done. I knew that. I'd seen, heard and been a part of it. I stopped to contemplate. Fixed on the same spot I always used. Particularly after those times: a shady deal, an encounter or an issue to be resolved on behalf of my old employers... and so again, I became fixed to that spot, gripping the bars as time stopped for me to wait on the crossroads before me.

Stop, go back, go to the pub... or jump the fuck in and forget it all, leaving it all behind me.

Rumours had circulated for decades: an age-old psychopath preyed on the lost, the drunk and lonely as they walked those paths by the waterways at night. They pushed people in, held them under and pushed them from the safety of the sides as they reached out helplessly. Until they were done for. Maybe there was one. A psycho. If there was, they couldn't compete with the numbers of lost souls added by the gangs. The unnamed, shamed, and those punished for taking a skim, not taking one or just being in the wrong place.

I didn't intend on adding to it that night.

The last time I'd lent on those railings and felt the metal dig into my hands, with space I'd made to think, I'd decided to testify against those gangs, the mob and Mr. Big. I knew I'd be kicked out. I knew I'd lose my life even as my heartbeat on but my prospects stopped.

I never thought I'd be back on that same spot. The police neither. The city needed cleaning up. And like the waterways, they needed dredging to expose the skulls, shoes and lives they'd fucked over for evermore—I'd send them all down this time. My ruminations drifted. I shifted focus back to the explosive point at hand. The one that was both my conscience, past and purpose; to solve the boy's case. I followed the flyer, and aimed back at The Boardwalk club in the Arches.

Everyone's got to be somewhere; even if it's nowhere.

10

Slight Return

I PASSED THROUGH an Irish bar on a corner by Canal Street, paying my respects with a pint of Guinness and a double Jameson. It'd be rude not to.

A group of shiny security bomber jackets glinted at me in the one faded light, as I neared the red brick archway entrance to The Boardwalk.

The punters; a mass of mainly shirted men, and those that were barely men in T-shirts. They spewed in and out of the place, holding fags and pints. In constant flux, with a swagger as if their pockets were being held down by giant weights in their pockets. This happened whilst supposed giant testicles meant they had to keep a constant bouncing gait. They swung along, arching their legs with each step. These steps carried the mass of constant drunken momentum and excitement: for a band coming on, a girl they almost talked to, the next song, their new jeans and... the drugs they were about to come up or down on. It was a fake-branded mess of Ben Sherman, Fred Perry and Adidas.

The closer I got, the more I felt like an impersonator of my past self; that I shouldn't have dared the attempted slight return. Those on the doors and in the shadows would think so too— so brazen of me, foolish of me, suicidal—so dead of me...

Having expected a rough-down, frisk or interrogation by the door staff; there was none of it. I seemed to glide in unnoticed—

a ghost. Just a dull-dirty-shade-of-nearing-middle-age that's too much of a nothingman for that self-obsessed night-life crowd. The bouncers were blinkered, distracted as well.

I went under the radar amongst the rest of the herd as they all tried desperately to be the exact opposite to me. Wanting to be noticed, they pranced around like apes; hoping to be the next King Monkey.

A group of three girls, a rarity in amongst the dick swingers, conveniently distracted and pussy-blinded the door staff to my presence. And so they let me pay and drift effortlessly in—a mere faded image of my gangland past.

A vaulted ceiling and an arch of more red brick continued inside like a giant cancerous brick lung. It heaved to and fro with the city's hum, its people and traffic outside. The cavern of a space expanded and contracted as the people inside got more drunk, intoxicated and high. They were its tumours, getting more terminal with each passing moment. They stuck to the walls, bar and floor.

Like all nights like these, at some point I was sure it was going to kick-off. I added to the smoke that engulfed the space and all those spaces between. It was on the bricks, mortar and our clothes.

Small and claustrophobic, there was a bar at one end and a stage at the other. Toilets doors complete with drug touts and people-watchers were to the side. A cloud hung above and occasionally reached down thickening above our heads—an inverse drowning.

I listened hard through the background hum, the shouts, chatter, music and the sound checks by technicians and roadies on the stage. I was listening for a clue, a break and a connection. I was also wary of any underworld scout that might have it in for me, or a runner that might suddenly spot, mark and then disappear to tell others of my whereabouts.

I leant at the end of the bar and waited.

Three student lads barged in and up to the bar by me. They giggled, bobbing about with a pre-loading of cheap spirits and discounted booze from their nights' run-up to this point. From then on for them it would all slow to a blur and be forgotten by the next morning. Their blood too young for hangovers, they'd reset and be back on it by the afternoon.

There was a short, tall and mid-height one. Everyone's dress code had merged into a soup of silhouettes, shadows, stains and blurs and they were no different. Despite their efforts before coming out; preening, ironing and dusting off—everyone had faded to black.

'How'd we get away with that and get in…?' the tall one asked. He took out what looked like a floral Dorothy Perkins style old-lady type dress. It emerged from behind his belt line as he put it scrunched up on the bar.

'Mental, totally mental…' the shorter one continued and took out a roll of carpet tape, putting it next to the dress.

'Yeah… Holy-fuck-a-saurus!' The mid-height one finished and added a Stanley knife to the pile.

'They found it all and just let us in… I don't get it?' the tall one went.

'You could've carried a fucking bazooka in here and they wouldn't give a fuck…' I interjected. Their celebrations and disbelief shattered. All the student prank crap in it was nothing amongst the real gangster shit going on in the shadows.

'What?' they said in unison, turned and half jumped at the sound and sight of me. I rearranged my slouch on the bar and stood upright.

'They really don't give a fuck. As long as you aren't carrying drugs.'

'But everyone's off their tits,' the low-level one said, and I sensed he was the older, more confident of the three clowns.

'Off their tits on gear bought, supplied, dealt, confiscated and then re-sold on by the door-apes working here,' I said, 'It's their own supply… Come in here with your own or a competing gang's to pass on or pollute their profits, their circulation—they'll have you floating face down in the canal.'

'Three double whiskeys and three pints of cider,' the mid-height one said to the barman, in a hurried urge to escape the crazy guy pissing on their joviality. It was as if a bucket of cold water had just been thrown on them. I felt guilty having momentarily sobered their drunkenness.

'Ice in the cider,' the tall one said, finishing the order. I sensed they'd already escaped my harsh wake-up call. They formed unison in a private joke—embodied in a quote from a film.

With nails in my heart and stomach I tried to engage further with them. Socialising had become a forgotten or never present tool to me but I appreciated it had a point. Even if not for the reason people traditionally went about it. It was a necessary evil; a stepping stone for getting me from A to B. I'd go from one side to another. Given choices, I would have normally bridged the interaction—avoiding it altogether. Sink or swim, I was on a case. Actually, two. Entwined together in the worst possible way—I was sure. I needed to be in the room, integrate with it and to feel what the low down was.

'What's it all for then. The dress, knife, tape?' I asked… Then, was interrupted by the band as they walked onto the stage to a rumbled of reserved applause. The kind that only comes from a time, place and band where everyone's too cool to express themselves fully—not least of all the band themselves. The music and listeners communicated in metaphors, similes, grunts, stares and swagger. Their attitudes were louder than the first chords they would play. Louder than bombs.

'It's our mate's birthday, we're gonna strip him and tape him to the lamp post outside...' they all seem to shout in unison, proud of themselves. They squeezed the words out with a glance at me then back at the stage waiting for the first notes to come.

'We've cut the arse out,' the tall one said, smug. He laughed as he fingered the torn dress.

With a dull E-Minor chord it all kicked off from the stage—as much as it ever would. Then came a feeling sweeping over me, a disappointment, that rose up uninvited. Regardless of the lack of effort by band and crowd the music did sum up certain unsaid truths of the city and the times. A sadness, a frustration and a wanting from those without us all hung in that air. I realised turning to the stage as the lights moved, that the band was the one from the poster I'd ripped and carried. I recognised the vacant looks, eyebrows and mop tops. And then I saw the drummers kit proudly displaying the shoe shop, or women's clothes shop sounding name that didn't fit their swagger. Like all bands and brands, if they made it, the word would lose all connotations other than the ones they'd made for themselves. They'd own the word and the letters; so would those who bought into it.

A few of the girls that were outside got in and gravitated towards the aspiring prankster threesome. They must have been on the same course at University, in the same halls of residence or related as the pairing of them all together seemed unlikely. The girls were first division. The boys were third or fourth—or hadn't qualified. I saw their bond as the girls ordered pints, shots and pulled eagerly at the arse-cut-out dress as it dangled over the bar's edge.

In what I guessed was a break in the band's set another joker arrived. I saw his long blond hair as he grabbed two of the girls by the arse: marking his arrival. His unwanted melee of kisses were met by simmering mixed chemistry—irritation and jealousy by each girl; pissed at not being singled out. That, and with it came an unmistakable familiarity. One of the girls displayed a lingering hold of just plain irritation at having to play along with the ladette shit that didn't quite fit, and that she had done it anyway. She held out, not laughing it off. They all did. Except one. The same one I was sure he'd fucked with last. Her nervous escape of expressed sympathy was awkward and singled her out. The others have had time to get over the prick a bit—to hold their own self-respect.

'He-he,' the blonde lad laughed at his own joke or action that hadn't been told yet, and the others politely went along now. Still with an underlying resentment of the effort it took. 'He-he' he giggled and I felt like knocking him out again, harder.

He went on like that for some time. He desperately wanted someone to ask what the joke was.

No one did, no one cared. The band came back on.

Shrugging his shoulders he picked a wrapper from his pocket and dumped it to the bar. It slowly unravelled to reveal an empty malt loaf wrapper. As it finished opening I looked over to a number of men who stumbled out from the gents' toilet door; shocked and shaking their heads. I picked up the wrapper and went over.

The band played a soundtrack to my slow-motion approach into whatever lay behind the door. Another shocked, almost-about-to-puke man stumbled out. He looked white and I feared the worst. I walked into the gents to see two men at one side of the room in true horror holding their faces, and looking at the metal urinal. I walked up to it, expecting to see a hand, a foot an ear, or an eye.

At the end of the urinal, blocking the piss flow trap was a

perfectly formed turd. Too perfect and cylindrical in form by all accounts. Almost a foot long and healthy. Not that I'd have known anymore.

'How...why?' one of them said from behind me. I noticed there wasn't a stink. I now saw the joke. I pissed over the fake turd and threw the malt loaf wrapper over my shoulder at the quivering spectators.

'No shit,' I said.

I shook, buttoned up and walked back out to the music. The band played another strange soundtrack for my walk back to the bar. I managed to roll and light a cigarette as the student girls looked on at me, and the three student lads tried not to. The blonde lad had already got distracted by another part of the room; like a hyperactive Labrador he'd fucked off to screw someone else's leg.

I took the rest with me into the night.

11

Atrocity Exhibition

I'D SOMEHOW BECOME an unwilling mentor; a priest for the night. Dressing in black and giving off a sense of aloofness all added to it. As I left each bar; the students followed.

I let the evening fall like that.

I knew it wouldn't last, it wasn't an act; like the band. And they'd eventually tire of my genuine demeanour. Unlike the prancing peacocks on stage with faked baggage and swagger.

I questioned them about the S.I. symbol and the boys fall—and the jump or push that preceded it. It was safe enough. They were just tourists there. As long as their courses and student loans lasted. Unmarried into the darker side of the city, the gangs, the violence. A safe line of questioning…to be met with naive answers.

My type, the gangs and bar staff didn't normally mix with these students. The rough sides looked down on those who weren't scarred by the city. They'd been told by university lecturers: keep a safe distance, be wary—stay alive—stay away from the tracksuit-chavs and runners.

There sure was some irony: a lot of the students were from the same background, and were making something for themselves. Pushed out of the estates by parents trying to create opportunities for them. They were from similar backgrounds. It could have been me too; a studier of books rather than a brawling, stewed P.I. writing them.

Maybe it was a destiny and I was always meant to end up there, scribbling the book out. And the girl left behind on the platform...a love lost, but not to fade away.

There was more than a pint of that irony in the inverted snobbery from the working classes towards the students. They all dressed down. Aiming for an appearance like the bands they saw on stage, on their TV screens and in the streets. All parties were trying to be something they weren't. They didn't mix but were more alike than they realised; the students, gangs, door staff and runners.

OUTSIDE IN THE glare of the street lamps one of the girls, darker than most, tried it on. I blanked her. Adding fuel to the short- lived cool aloof smoking image they had painted over me.

'Jeez, what's your problem—am I not for you?' she said—she wasn't used to being turned down. Not for a kiss... for anything; more used to the liberal student meat markets and The Roxy up the road—where it was actions first then ask if they're interested and fancy a drink later.

'I'm already in love,' I said.

'Then what's her problem—being stuck with you?' she poked at me.

'Guess she can't find a better man,' I admitted, thinking of Cherry. In my head she was still on that train platform, a pedestal in my head—the image was vivid, not faded yet. Not enough to take a cheap thrill. Not from *this* girl...

I walked us further into the night. Without them knowing the potential pains that awaited.

'Where' we going?' one of the lads asked.

'The only club there is,' I said. I sounded grave. I couldn't help it. Its history was woven with mine in bad blood. I muttered its name.

'Is that still going—I thought the police had killed it?' another lad said.

'They won't stop until it's flattened. Even if it's rebuilt as flats it'll be in the canal, roads and pavements—it is the city,' I addressed the congregation.

My crazy-talk got nervous giggles—my facade was cracking with each step. Real-life was too much for them—they craved escapism and had the rest of their lives to wake up.

They shrugged shoulders and got distracted. Another group came alongside; with the 'birthday boy'. They meant to dress him up, in an arse-cut-out dress and tie him to a lampost. Part of me wanted to see how it played out.

I meant to question them more. Before I took them to the last standing church to true faith in the city. There'd be other questions, answers, conflict and memories in there… Maybe the S.I. symbol's artist had just ripped off the club's coding they'd used—maybe not though and the whole seedy mess was inter-connected. And, Mr. Big just piggybacked the whole movement and had milked it for cash—like everyone else.

One of the girls ran up and whispered in my ear: 'If she doesn't get to you I will…' she was very matter of fact.

Welcome to the late nineties on the turn of the 21st Century where the hunters had become prey and the girls had become the boys: 'ladettes'. The shift felt healthy for a while; a rebalance. Like a boat righting itself; having tilted too much the other way before and then trying to right itself. Or a boxer hit back on his heels before returning to balance to strike back. It'd been too much another way for too long and the stronger female sexes were revelling in the opportunity. Regaining some ground on the playing field.

'I'm gonna fuck you if she doesn't—one of us… is gonna…

FUCK you.'

'Don't bother, I'll be lucky to make it out of there alive,' I said.

MANCHESTER WAS AN idea; a concept. An ideal in people's heads crafted together by bands, labels, agents and the smoky piss and wind blowing around the city that fuelled them all. It was both false memory and real; a state of mind bred-out in the attitude of the clubs, music, weather, buildings, beer and water. It had a background hum; a noise that wouldn't quieten. The waterways, roads, industry (dead and dying), cars and pedestrians omitted a vibration that added to the cacophony of it—all in a constant state change, jostling, jarring… The club was at the centre of all of this. A loudspeaker to channel the minds and souls. David Coulter, the painter, sums it up well; impressionistic blurs of light, water, vibrancy and most of all the noise—you can't stop the noise. If he was painting water lilies his pieces could easily be confused with Monet. But because it was Manchester and Salford, there was a gritty realism for the eyes that Monet wasn't alive to play with on canvas. So the bands, Lowry and Coulter played with it and made the ideas, past the rain and smog, for real. We walked through the beautiful noise.

The melee of late-night revellers added to it, albeit in a less sincere way than some of us. I worked at it like this most times of day. There was a lot of pleasure tourists out to get out of it, their faces and for any reason. Turning up once a week they'd devour more than their fair share. Flocking in from the surrounding cities and further, they'd come to worship at the church of urban escapism—they made me sick to think about it too much.

The same sorts had stood by, pilled-up and out of it when I used to work there. I rescued the girl from the club, the drugs and the city as I had put her one soul above the rest. I tried to do right and was turned down and ostracised, targeted and stained for evermore. As I carried her out I left them all behind, until now as I returned with the students.

As we walked, my thoughts hammered it home to me: why go back? Why be back at the epicentre... the crash site and the source of all the pain? Was I actually suicidal? With a death wish? Surely remnants of Mr Big's gang and their peers would still be clinging to the sides of whatever was left of the place. Or, was I facing all that held me back head-on... to get it over with and take a future with Cherry sooner rather than later. And to give M. Pampelmousse her story, the one she deserved.

This story.

THE INTERIOR OF the place screamed 'WARNING' from yellow and black striped columns that held its high ceiling. There was a warning about the bands, about the drugs, the gangs... and if you were like me—a warning against ending up working the door, saving a girl and becoming a moving target. Most of all... there was a warning against returning.

We didn't see any of that, joined the queue and waited. We wouldn't see any of it for the mass of writhing, heaving and squeezing. The people, smoke and spills reached up to the baffles on the ceiling and back down to the warning striped pillars.

I resisted the temptation to describe to the students what waited for them.

I ran over the layout in my head—a refresher in case I needed it in a hurry: the giant steel doors, raised stage to the right, the main bar to the back left. A DJ booth to the left overlooked the dance floor. Stairs down to a basement bar and other stage. Toilets to the back; not enough for the capacity of the club— there used to be a plastic tub in the shadows and sometimes the one in the kitchen if they let me in; the overflow to piss in.

I only knew the details and positions existed because I'd seen it with the lights on, and with no people—just me and the echoes of the future memories—the memories of the case that had got me expelled.

'Why are we going to this place?' one of the girls asked as we joined a queue going up and around the corner. We'd joined it on the bridge over the canal and for a moment as I looked through its steel beams as I pushed down the urge to jump in. The canals weaved under the roads of the city like veins and it felt natural to want to join them now. All but for a pressing moral mission for the boy's mother. And like the girl I carried from the club all them years ago something had become more important to me. Flashes of hope with Cherry and my writing added layers of texture as my own noise and hum drowned out the city's own malaise over me.

'You don't have to go in,' I stated to all of them. 'I promise— it won't be boring if you do though. By the time we're done in there, you'll have seen parts of the city they don't warn you about on campus or in a prospectus. You'll have had more than your fill of the city.'

'Melodramatic fuck,' one of the girls said. If it had come from one of the guys I'd have slapped them back into line— sobered them up.

My words felt out to her; to touch a nerve instead: 'I used to work here. There won't be a welcome party. Most likely they're gonna want to rip me in two... Don't stand too close to me in there, or be seen talking to me as we get closer to the front of the queue. I've seen what they do to girls they like in there—and even worse to the ones they don't...'

'Where's the fucking police then?' a bean-pole looking guy asked nervously.

'The gangs rule this, not the police.'

'Then what are you up to, you crazy bastard?' another girl chipped in.

'Sometimes the police need a little help to do the stuff they know they need to... but can't.'

'I thought you were a writer?' another girl asked opening my coat to reveal the top of a Moleskin and pen.

'I'm writing for her. Writing to reach her. Them both... All three of them come to think of it—the holy fucking trinity, plus one.'

'Who?'

'Therapist, agent and Cherry. And a girl that died in there."

'Therapist? What the fuck? And who's Cherry? Dead girl—what the fuck?' they muttered in unison.

'Who's Cherry?' I repeated out loud—to myself. And, as I did, I wondered: 'am I going to make it out alive... to find out what she means to me?'

12

The Perfect Kiss

I FELT SURE the bouncers would clock me as we got closer and tried to distance myself from the students—for their own safety.

There'd been such a turnover of staff since I'd fucked up the rota for them, by spilling them to the police, that no one I recognised was working at the front. The gangs had sure loosened their grip on the place already. In its death throes already—on its last legs. Soon it would be a block of flats and every lasting memory in the fixtures, fittings and dance floor ebayed off to the highest bidders.

Those giant metal doors creaked open.

An uncertain look from the heavies let me know I was clocked to a degree; tagged as a possible future issue—but I was let in anyway. It wouldn't be long for that issue to show.

Inside the masses swelled around on and off the stage, using it as an extra dance floor, as it raised up to my right. The main dance floor, also filled, continued below the stage.

This foot or two between the stage and the main dance floor was the distance the girl fell when I used to work there. I'd picked her up, all those years ago. She was wearing a little white slip—night clothes really. After a bad pill, she'd fallen from the raised stage section with one leg left on it as her other searched for the floor below.

Like in the film Alien, a spray of blood instantly went up her front… She was ripped and torn apart by the place. No one stopped to care, but me. And it stopped the path I was on for evermore.

The night she'd fallen, the revelling had gone on. All were ignorant and sedated by the scent of their own demise. The DJ had spun his thing in a high up booth as one of the bar girls knelt in front of him, as her mouth… did her thing. The broken glass she knelt in would give her a permanent reminder. And the bar staff had continued handing out what they believed were free drinks—no such thing.

Someone always pays.

And… the dance floor still writhed on as the band downstairs in the basement played on too. All were so wasted, each of them played a different song at the same time. As I tried to reach the struggling girl a bouncer ran through and past me in the opposite direction, pulling a knife out of an arse cheek. All commonplace shit for any night of the week back then. Except for the blood-covered girl at the base of the stage in the centre, fitting and foaming at the mouth. And, me skating upstream on thin ice against them all to get to her.

Little did anyone know that the girl was the epicentre to a bomb that was about to drop—a keystone to the whole lot that I was about to pull loose. The pill she'd bought, likely from one of the gangs, or one of us on the door, was the fuse.

It was lit, burnt out and I was the powder about to go off. Now… with the students:

I'D RETURNED TO find the place showing the final death throes of a dying beast before the tax man, gangs, bands and record labels took whatever was left—maybe it always was that pained. Nearly free booze and entry had the place filled with students, pretend gangsters and clubland tourists reminiscing about a time that hadn't really existed, other than in the magazines and heads of those that had created it. And all of them, as before, looked for their last bite from an already empty plate; leeches, parasites and infections the lot of them—pollutants of a party they started but were no longer invited to.

As I reminisced and walked through the smoke and strobes, invisible monsters hid and looked from behind each corner, pillar and moving body that turned. More ghosts than actual threats to me. I'd wanted to throw the lights on the place like I had in court—to see what I was dealing with—weigh up my chances.

I wanted them to bring it on… and get everything out into the open. And cut to the fucking chase.

Looking around I clocked everything and everyone up close, even if they didn't notice me. None of them looked back. They were too engrossed, taken by the rhythm, into themselves, entranced and focussed on the direction of their next fixes.

The background hum built to a noise, a cacophony as all aspects of the environment jarred in and out of unison. The DJ's tune was the finishing skin to it all; a wallpaper. The racket peaked and then fell… Then there was just static: white noise. The spotlights stopped moving and the strobes stopped flashing. Then they were all switched off, putting us in total darkness. All but a for a dull glow from the moon through the skylights high above us. People climbed from the stage as a strobe started to flash again. And with it a familiar figure entered from the darkest shadows at the rear of the stage. The strobe staggered his walk as he jolted to the front like a bad dream.

He took the mic. It was Jerry.

Jerry was an ex-TV presenter and hanger-on from the days when the club had something to hang on to.

He said: 'Hard-core party people. Hello and welcome...' and the crowd murmured approval. 'Welcome to this: your shrine,' he went on, raising his arms, and they all swayed on his words, 'The decanted pot of your shit we like to call...HOME.' they stirred again in anticipation, 'A cathedral to true faith,' and the mass frenzy was primed... 'Welcome to our new order.' Again they loved it. 'Welcome to...' and he paused for dramatic effect, and he got it from all... but me, 'Your fucking CHURCH!' And the crowd went wild.

I resented having to listen to this shit from an ex-C list celebrity. One who wouldn't have got on the guest list back in the day. I wouldn't have let him in—times had changed.

'We love you all!' he said and they calmed down, 'And we love each other...' again a pause for effect, 'ALL. BUT. ONE.' and with this he silenced them.

I stirred. Now I was unsettled.

A realisation—I wasn't as invisible as I'd thought.

A spotlight went around me and people nearby stepped out of my light. It was left to me. Alone. Then he pointed me out. He told them I was the bastard son of the place, now returned... How I was the prodigal child that was never wanted.

Then it came: as I was transfixed to the spot, a familiar hard barrel of a gun pushed to the back of my head.

With the cold metal against my spine—free will and my options dissolved. I was walked out of the limelight.

As if nothing had happened, the music re-started and with it the writhing masses too. Their zombie-like moves were less a dance celebration; more a watered-down passionless iota of what the place used to move like.

I was forced up the stairs; my face used to open the DJ booth door.

'Son of the club... That's a fuckin' joke. A walking fucking abortion more like,' a familiar shape turned and said from the decks in front of me. She sat, grinning, and waved my gun-carrying escort to move outside. And then the door was shut on us. Leaving us in the cupboard of a room. It used to be the epicentre of such dreams; now it rapidly turned into a nightmare.

Teri became a good DJ, studied the best, but her standards must have been slipping.

'I swear I could have recognised your sets. You used to be good, trained by the best,' I said, glancing at the scar on her knee. I left my gaze there long enough—she knew what I meant by *trained.*

'Shut it John. You're not welcome here!' Like I needed her to say that.

'What is it with you? You suicidal or something?'

'Maybe… Just maybe.'

'You're safer here. They'll rip you apart down there… You're like a fucking wounded rat anyway.'

'Feels like the city's been waiting to do that since I got back—to break me.'

'Bollox,' she winked, 'it missed you though too… eh?' she whispered. And she leant in. I could smell the vodka Redbull as her lips parted. She went for a kiss…

This time, I didn't resist.

Cherry is all I wanted. But, I needed Teri on my side. I reciprocated enough to be polite. It had been a long time and we had history, or so I thought. Enough for parts of me to miss her too. We'd ridden those decks, this floor and broken a chair or two back then.

A kiss was all I thought.

… But a kiss is never all it is.

'Sorry John, didn't think you'd go as quietly as this. I expected… I hoped… for something bigger. For you to finish what you'd started.' And a tear welled in one of her eyes.

'Someone wants to make an example of you,' she continued. And as she leant back I looked down at my leg which stung, then back up to her hand...

It held an empty syringe.

'Night night,' she whispered again, and she blew me a kiss 'goodnight... and goodbye.'

I faded to black.

13

Transmission

TAXI FOR SIX:

'Wakey wakey sunshine,' a voice broke through the dark veil of sedation and deceit.

A slap followed, then a punch cracking my jaw—finishing the wake-up call.

My right hand was taped to a steering wheel and my left to a gear stick. In the rear view mirror, I saw four of the students. Their hands were taped. And despite being roughed up, bruised and beaten up, they were belted in—like safety mattered.

I became aware of a rope around my neck. I looked back, craning my neck. It came from a rope reel behind the passenger seat. The other end went past one of the quivering girls, out the back window to a lampost where it was tied off.

'Now John... you know how this goes, don't you?' came a familiar voice from a past, from a fellow doorman (and ex-military heavy). Some of them used to have my back—I guess this one wasn't one of them.

'It's simple—child's play really. I'll spell it out for those in the back. The children who you've dragged into this fucking mess. They can talk about what they've seen. Put it in their next papers for Uni'... It's like this: I'm gonna put this gun to your head,' and he did, 'and you're gonna drive... It's up to you how fast, or how slow. But a few things are for sure. Your neck is gonna fuckin' break. And the police are gonna put it down to suicide. And if these students want to live out their loans, they'll say enough to spread the word, which won't mean shit in court. After all, John… the city hates you! You know it. There's nothing here for you anymore. The note you leave, this note,' and he patted his shirt pocket, 'will say you came back to make amends. To make up for hurting what you loved most—who won't buy that shit?'

Divulging the background; being there on unofficial approval of the police. And on a case to find why a boy who had jumped from a tower block would've meant nothing to him. As far as he was concerned I'd come back, to check my work on the place. And that Mr Big was locked up. That his legacy had started to rot to hell—he'd be part right at that.

I looked straight ahead and put the car in gear.

I revved the engine hard, as my eyes blackened over again. 'Oh, he's keen to get on with it—righty then, off we go,' he announced, rubbing the gun between his hands in excitement. 'Buckle up nippers,' he said. His jovial put-on posh tone emphasised the fact he'd done this set piece we were to play out before… And way too much.

In the back, they looked in sheer terror—their fear at being witness to pure evil.

The tape over their mouths stifled silent screams.

Then their eyes widened, red and through tears, and then they were squeezed shut tight. As if to try to awaken from a nightmare. One of the worst to be in; lucid and from the dark side of real-life. A side they wouldn't have known if it weren't for me.

Through the windscreen and the rain, resting in the droplets on the car's bonnet I could see what had become a familiar revenant; my alter-ego, sidekick and reasoning to draw on the strengths of my past and history—the Viking. There was no fear there, in him. His eyes were wide and cold: fierce.

I looked in the rear view mirror at myself as my eyes widened. Rivers of past pains pushed through my veins. Without fear, a force of nature, about to charge at the enemy. I looked back at the droplets on the front of the car and they'd turned black, like blood in the moonlight—like my eyes.

I revved some more. Clenched my jaw tight.

'Easy,' he said, attempting to seize back an unseen control back away from me, 'a little keen to end your misery aren't you Johnny-Boy?'

I said: 'People make mistakes. First one is thinking they won't.'

'Cryptic bull-shit,' he said, 'And before you go—here's a little word from our sponsor.'

Acid rose in the pit of my gut.

He slipped a tape into the recorder and pressed play.

It hissed a sinister white noise. Then *he* kicked in: Mr Big, talking real slow; menacing. He paused when he didn't need to, and he breathed time-wasting sighs. He relished the letters, words, and the time he took from me with each one. He knew he had me and that I was on a cliff's edge, with time running out, and his words, the last I'd hear, pierced me from the tape machine.

He took his time, stole my last moments knowing they'd last an eternity to me.

The tape hissed:

'You know John—it was always going to be like this. You did this to us. All of us. And you know how it goes Johnny-Boy; do unto others as you would... yeah what- ever-the-fuck—you sanctimonious fuck! Choke on this

rope, your self-made halo, slipped into the place where it belongs now hasn't it—you CUNT! You don't know how much pleasure it gave me to write your suicide note. And before you do go… I thought you should know what it says…'

My heart pounded—breaking through my ribcage. My ears echoed each beat.

'It says… you sold her that pill—The one that killed her. Funny that, isn't it? And it says… that's why you tried to save her—your fuckin' guilt. They'll believe it too… won't they John?

So, it'll free me and the boys back up to get back on with the supply and demand. The club and city demand it… and we WILL supply it. And you John… you'll be labelled a drug pushing, fucked up SAS drop out. And best of all: A GIRL KILLER. And d' you know what I'm going to do as a passing gift, just for you? Once a year, on the day she died, we'll drop a really nasty one in the bag and make sure it's taken. You see John, you tried to save one bitch… and we'll take one more each year in your name. Johnny's pill—a little passing gift. Might even put a little logo of your face on it. And do you know what John? That's not even the best part…

(He gasped with excitement.)

My heart pounded some more in my chest, racing on each hissing word. My eyes were wide; unblinking. If I was ever to have a heart attack—it'd have been right then. The adrenaline had me focussed.

Then came his final words for me:

'You will tell them in your note that you spiked her, and that you were going to rape her. That's why you spiked her. You thought it was a roofie. But in the end, you fucked it right up.'

My face dropped; my blood past boiling point. I was adrenalised—to the max.

'Now, Joe… chew that fucking tape up. Like a good boy. And I'll see you on the other side.'

He ejected it. Dragged out the tape and he ate at it. He tried to swallow some, coughed and coldly looked ahead. He threw up out the window; dropping the casing with it. Then, he coughed some more, clearing his throat.

He pointed, stabbing at the air with the gun for me to go. My heart, breath, rage and fury were in perfect balance. The

Viking's image shone on the road ahead of me…

I pulled at the steering wheel with clenched fists. I used the fake shrunken skull gear knob to force the car into gear, again.

The car screeched on.

People do make mistakes. And the first one is thinking they won't.

Joe's mistakes included: forgetting that I'd driven this car before. It was used by the doormen and club odd-jobbers as a run-around. I'd fitted this shitty fake skull gear knob too. He also didn't figure I knew there were about 29-30 meters between lamp posts on this street in Longsight, Manchester.

I knew this because I'd sat in his seat to scare a young dealer before—stopping him before it was too late. He'd shat and pissed himself. It made the point. The rope Joe used was yachting rope. The basement store of the club was full of it from when it used to be a showroom. It was 16 millimetres in diameter and 100 meters long. That's how I knew... when to stop... before it was too late... Enough to scare the young dealer I'd caught back in the day. And that's how I knew my timing. I also knew I could pull the gear knob free. I'd screwed it on myself. And I knew that when I did it would reveal a ten-millimetre diameter metal rod that I would sink into Joe's neck, cutting up sharply after I braked the car hard and his head hit the dash.

Joe's final mistake: belting everyone in but himself.

I braked hard between the final lamp posts. Joe flew forward into the dash. His body snapped back, spraying the roof with crimson. Pulling the knob free of the gear stick, I buried the metal spike into his neck. Arterial blood sprayed, covering the inside of the passenger side windscreen. The legs, feet and faces of those in the back took a deep red Jackson Pollacking too.

His hand holding the gun dropped limp.

I pulled the car calmly over. And got the students out, un-taping them so they could throw up.

I lit a cigarette and looked at the stars. The Plough was there: Odin's Wain.

And again, for the time being, the Viking would rest.

14

What Do You Want From Me?

3.30 PM IS too late in the day to make plans. And too early to execute one. Caught up in no man's seconds, and trapped by no woman o'clock. Sartre said as much and who was I to question. At some point in time I rolled from the sofa to the floor, and from the floor to the bathroom. I went to flush and got no response.

There was a carrier bag in the cistern.

A sorry looking black PVC box of cassette tapes had been weighing it down. The previous occupant had wanted them found, but not by a cursory sweep of the flat by the police. Or by the cleaners. They wanted them found by whoever was to move into the Caretaker's flat next.

I lay on the sofa with a bastard behind the eyes. I drained the bag and opened the box. I thought it was just about as bad a music collection could get.

Then, I noticed some redemptive titles. Most had Vinyl Exchange 'reject' stickers on them. A second-hand record shop didn't even want them. The tapes, all originals, had masking tape over their ends to enable someone to re-record over them. The same tape had been used to retitle the cases.

Black smudged ink capitals crudely reworded the artists beneath:

TAPE 1: *Black Sabbath was retitled 'Nine Inch Nail'.* **TAPE 2 :**

Dire Straits' 'Brothers In Arms' became 'Black Bacon'.

TAPE 3: Queen II had become 'Broken'.

TAPE 4: Fleetwood Mac's 'Tango In The Night' was 'What Do You Want From Me?'

TAPE 5: Meat Loaf's 'Bat Out Of Hell' was renamed 'When The Lights Go Down'.

TAPE 6: Led Zeppelin IV was now 'Vulgar Pussycat'. **TAPE 7:** Simply Red's 'Picture Book' was retitled 'Wonder Lust.'

TAPE 8: Nirvana 'Bleach', had become 'Downer'.

A note in the box directed me to a small flatbed tape recorder. The type you'd find in a cheap police interview.

Under the sofa there's a loose tile.
Lift it and there's a safe without a keyhole. The code is 6969.
Your head's already way past the rabbit hole.
So long, A Friend.

Collapsing back into a haze, I recounted my steps of the night before. I blinked tight, reopened my eyes, making sure I wasn't in a bad dream. I reached for the Black Sabbath tape. Or, 'Nine Inch Nail', as it was now known.

The player clunked open unsympathetically. I reached behind the sofa and grabbed a can to go with it and snapped the player back shut.

At first, it hissed emptiness. Then a voice started… empty, male and croaking like each word was a massive drain to expel. You could feel the painful void between each breath.

A nothingman talked from the past at me:

'I don't know if this fucking job has taken me and my soul—or if I have no soul… So therefore I took the sodding job… It feels like it's all *been so long—each moment here does that. The minutes and seconds become hours.*

I stare at peeling walls as they open up to me.

I've seen an eternity of worlds in each of the cracks and stains. There's adventure in this wood-chipped hell—it drags me further and further into the fabric of the place—hell. The people: the scum that chooses to live here are all the same. I've seen it: that look they have; as they become the building's puppets.

They come and go like rats. Never really here.

Never not here.

Fucking ghosts... and rats... the lot of 'em.

It's like when the drink has you. And the fog takes over.

No longer do I take the drink—now it takes me, or so it goes. That's this fucking building... No longer are we just in it. We've been too long in its shell and it has carved a space out inside of each of us...'

(Hiss - Crackle).

'The other day, this bitch had it in her—literally.'

(Feedback).

'She didn't even flinch. She had a bit of the place right in her. T'was poking right through her. It was only when she reached for her mail, the letter I was holding. Her sleeve went up—I saw it—right there, plain as sight. A fucking rusted NAIL. Right through her forearm it was. I didn't notice at first. Then she reached across the counter top. I heard it scraping on the top. And she wanted me to see. She pushed her arm and the nail harder into the worktop 'till it screeched out. She didn't though. She licked at her lips... winked at me too.'

'Like she wanted it—dirty cow.'

'Her arm had been bleeding. It'd dried and crusted over; she'd just left the nail in there. It was like she didn't care. She had formed a bond with her wound.

After she'd gone I puked in the basket—then wanked over it. I imagined touching the nail as I did it too—she'd like that. That's what I whispered to myself as I finished up over my sick. I pity the cleaner that'll empty it.'

'And me most of all.'

Black Sabbath kicked in without warning—snapping me to. And I stopped the tape and looked at the waste-basket…

The building had me now too. No nails though. Not yet. The cleaner arrived. I asked her about the previous caretaker.

She barked: 'dirty bastard'. I guessed it was directed at him and not me. She banged through the double doors with a bucket and mop and was gone.

I rang Cherry; told her about the night before: the car, club, students, lamp post. And the body to pick up if they hadn't already. With a gear stick through its neck. She went quiet, showing a personal side; true feelings slipping through the armour. Then, the professional side kicked in. Stone cold she insisted I'd be o.k. And that's was why I was there. To rattle cages. His cage. I pointed out I'd more than rattled them, nearly losing my own fucking head. Almost got some students done in too.

She brushed it off. As if confident in a conclusion we hadn't got to yet—but was sure of.

I felt her: torn between duty and love.

If our love hadn't had a chance to breathe.

I asked her about the caretaker. And held back the details of the tapes. I wanted free reign for now. I knew they were worth listening to.

Cherry's thoughts on the caretaker weren't as sympathetic: 'He was zero. No lead. A loser. He had nothing during questioning. Not on the boy. No history. Just a sorry fuck, stuck in a dead-end job.'

'Even so, I want to speak to him. Cover every base,' I said and kept my thoughts to myself—that I might have more in common with him than I'd like to admit. 'What about the girl too?'

'What girl?'

'The one in the clippings… the photo. Looks like she might have found him first, tried mouth to mouth, a little late…' I asked.

'Another exhausted dead end. If she wasn't due to be committed before, she sure as hell was after,' she said.

It felt like another obvious piece of the puzzle to me. The hive mindset of the building's inhabitants was a growing concern. The girl with the nail on the tape, testimony to it.

'Kissing a corpse will do that to you. Why don't you want me on the boy's case?'

'Did I say that? There's bigger fish to fry though. The boy committed suicide—leave it as that. For her… And get *him* (Mr Big)'

'She doesn't want it left. The boy's mam wants the truth. Besides *he's* an easy play. I'm just winding them up. They'll rip themselves apart soon enough.'

'Shame they didn't tie the rope around your balls… Getting a bit big aren't they?'

'Where did you send the girl?'

She told me where I could find the old caretaker: in The Black Horse pub. And, the girl: St Lawrence Hospital. There was no sympathy to be found in either place. Just places to hide the unwanted, mask, mute and sedate them—out of sight and mind—into oblivion.

15

Cast No Shadow

THE BLACK HORSE was a shithole. Locals and students propped up bars in each of its four rooms. The locals were drawn to the smell of cheap beer, the student's naivety, and their youth. And the students were scared and exhilarated by the locals in equal measure.

By the time the students had drunk enough to be brave enough; talking with the locals, everyone was pissed enough to entertain without much hassle. Unless that is, one tried to jump a round, or take a seat that wasn't theirs. Hell was waiting if they took someone's seat when they went for a slash.

My man, the Caretaker, was an easy spot. I took a drink, or three. Waited.

A skinny guy downed a pint of something green. Then vomited it straight back into the glass it came from.

A Northern student girl argued, slapping and shouting a lad in a Wonder Stuff t-shirt. The locals cheered them on—bloodthirsty. She went to glass him; playing up to the crowd.

Not a real glassing. Without conviction.

The hard rim of the glass cut into the lad's nose. Neither broke. An hour later they're all friends, again. They'd probably all end up sleeping together—who knows.

The locals, disappointed at the flaccid performance, offered constant advice on how to do real damage if they want to go at it again. Demonstrating how they'd gone at it all wrong. They parried out with dummy blows and bottle lunges.

The students faked some comradery… then cowered away.

He showed himself. Made visible through his inaction in the proceedings. A lack of verve. He stared into a dead-end space under a bar top—I knew I had my man.

'Last orders,' the barman faked. They all knew it was for show. The blacked-out windows and thick curtains hadn't been opened in decades. This hole had never shut. 'Seriously I've lost my licence for good this time… I'm shutting up shop, no more,' he conceded. And after the third attempt, he said: 'fuck it' and told us to help ourselves. He didn't want the brewery or receivers to take anything.

Ironically, the mood turned more civilised at the prospect of self-service and free beer and spirits. Well… until the optics, bottles, and taps were emptied. I pocketed a bottle of Bell's. Took it and two tumblers to my target.

'I've got a real shit job. In a fucked-up place… The toilet doesn't flush. I bet you can guess where it is,' I said.

He looked up through sobering eyes.

A familiar depth, pain and sorrow swelled in him. 'How'd you find me?'

'Not hard. We're not far off being each other are we? What services were you?'

'How d' you know, or care?'

'You think you deserve a job like that. A demeaning piece of nothing. A gift to yourself. It's penance after you'd done things you hated. In other people's names, orders or whatever and are ashamed of it—I can smell it a fuckin' mile off…'

'Yeah?' he sniffed.

I slid him a large measure. 'Yeah. You see… That's me too.' I poured myself one.

'You a Pig?'

'Worse.'

'Really?' he grinned into his free drink before knocking it back.

'Yes... I'll think nothing of smashing your head right in here and now, free of the paperwork. If... I think you've earned it.'

'You must be ex-SAS then. No one else would be so sure of themselves... Assuming a weaker opponent,' he said into an empty glass.

'Just sounding you out.' I poured him another.

'Get to the point. Is it the boy, or the building you're wanting to know about?'

'Both and anything else besides... The tapes... Vulgar Pussycat?' I quizzed and he slowly started to stand. As he did, I noticed he was shaking and one eye, the one that had been away from me, was welling up. The other continued looking. Intense. Red. Enraged.

'You found them then. It's not just me you know. Each sap who's worked there did one—they go way... way back,' he muttered, then said he was going for a slash.

He never returned.

And I felt a fool for believing he would.

I WENT BACK to the block of flats with the bottle, and put on his tape. Its title and timing made sense. The word 'Downer' fitted both his demeanour and the boy's fall. But... had he titled it in advance or after the fall?

Tape 8 *'Downer':*

'I see the fields of blood... those flames in the shadows. This is when I'm awake. When I'm asleep, it's worse. I still jump at the crack of the

stapler the damn postman uses, even though I've just handed him it.'

There's a shock in the lightning, and a fear of the rain... as it hits the window pane. It didn't end when I left the ricocheting bullets I'd ducked and dived from over there.'

It rains a lot here.' 'Lightning too.'

Manchester's war—it tortures me. My past falls from its clouds.'

I've done my fucking time for this country. Now, I do it again—as a prisoner of my memories. I'm tied to it. My history.'

I'll cut myself.'

To see if I'm still here.'

Then there was a pause. An intake of breath. My heart seemed to stop. I felt close to this sorry soul—not far from me at all; before the writing and cases had started to ease the pain.

He started up again:

(A deep breath).

I'm not quite as alone as I'm made to feel... I've seen them. The others. Scarred, cut and bruised too. They wear this all with smiles like badges of honour. It's all surface—no real feeling. There's too many of them been cut here in these flats. They're doing it to each other. I know it—the sick fucks.'

(Intake... gasps).

I've recorded over this same tape. Every day now.

Whatever's on it will be the last of me. It's like my life now; trying to rewrite over the memories each day.

Like it never happened.

But it's always... the same.

The day I check out or quit this, it'll be all that's left of me... '

In the background of the recording there's a loud thump, screaming and lots of shouting...

'What have those dumb fucks done now? Thrown another mattress out the windows again and hit someone or a car. The fuckin' Morons.'

...came the intense voice from the tape.

There was no fallen mattress. It was the boy. I could hear the screams on the tape. Louder than war.

Then, the girl's pain rang through, above it all.

I decided to visit her at St Lawrence; a psych hospital. I hoped their shared madness there wouldn't rub off on me... Or worse, mine on them.

16

Linger

I'D HEARD HER screams on the tape. And I'd seen her photo in the police file: those eyes carrying an infinity of love lost. That pain—frozen in time.

She was no different in her cell (the only name for it). She was made a prisoner in the moment of the boy's drop. Her eyes, like tunnels to nowhere, looked black; hollow and savage-looking. Staring out the window through a wall of rain. I knew she'd loved him. What else could have done that to her... only that can. Or fear. She sat in her little two-by-three-meter cell staring out into her memories.

I tried to break through but she was closed off. Sedated to hell. 'You knew Will? The boy that fell?'

I leant on the window ledge alongside her. Tried not to push her too hard. There's nothing to be gained by breaking what's already broken. Then it came out of me: 'What's all these stories about people hurting themselves in those flats? Did he... go... too far?'

'We've all taken it too far... no way back for us now,' she muttered as drool dripped from her lip, from the sedatives.

I kept staring out with her,

'We've played with pain and the Devil's tool-kit... In his own playground. There's no way back... We welcomed him in. Played his games. He's taken him—the soul goes down.'

'What?' I asked.

'There'll be more… Much, much more.'

'Is it to do with this.?' and I showed her a sketch of the S.I. letters I'd seen. She looked over at me, then down.

She smiled.

It was a dead and hollow thing.

She pressed her fingernail into the window ledge hard. She continued, pressed harder again. I was sure her nail would snap back any second exposing the flesh beneath. Then she put her other hand down the front of her jeans and started to rub at herself. Blood started from her nail. I grabbed her hand from the ledge and shouted for help.

For the first time as far as I could remember, I'd felt panic.

I was reminded of the other girl, from the first tape—the one with the nail in her arm.

I stewed over my visit. And rested up in the Old Pint Pot next door.

When I'd stopped shaking, I took out my notebook. The S.I. symbol looked back at me. It carried a weight now.

I wrote '=Sado-Intimacy'.

Then, I snapped my notebook, my thoughts, and what felt like the Devil's own branding tight shut.

17

Life's An Ocean

I DON'T KNOW how long I'd been leaning on the rails, looking at the iced-over canal. There was an eternity in its black misted over depths. My hands were stuck hard to the icy railings. The water held memories and secrets encapsulated tight shut behind an ice shield… Until the thaw that would inevitably come each year—releasing them.

Events and the drinks had caught up with me and brought me here.

Arms grabbed me. I didn't resist.

A strength within was weakened by my introspection. I was frozen by the same notions that had placed me at the canal side. A darkness of contemplation; fuelled by the force that had taken the girl's mind and the boy's life.

I felt blows, a blanket over my head and then more blows. A lift and a shove the land was gone. I was in the air.

I looked back from the ice to the point where I once stood. The chill froze my arse to the bone. Colder stares came from the canal side. They had my life in their hands. All five of them bent down and picked up bricks. Then they started to throw. Like shooting fish in a barrel; if they hit me I was hurt bad. If they missed and hit the ice, it'd break and I would go down anyway.

I covered my head as best I could, sliding and squirming as the melee went on. I looked down into the ice as it started to turn black. With blood. My blood.

Behind the wall of ice, through the infinity of time, my past and the inevitability of my future looked back at me from the other side; I saw The Viking—and I knew the journey I was about to take. This time he had a sombreness, a sympathetic acceptance in his eyes when once there was resilience, strength and vehemence.

The ice cracked, broke, wobbled, cracked apart and I went under: down.

I was stunned; wrapped in icy coldness.

With the adrenaline, some strength returned. I was awakened and spurred on by memories of all my past near-deaths—I'd hit through them all, to the other side and back again.

I took it in, and swam hard into the darkness.

I kept going into the blackness and avoided the light.

The icy cold waters had me in its inevitable embrace towards death. What was left of my oxygen was little and impure. The water bore a ton of my prior bad decisions in each stroke.

A dot appeared and then it became a disc. I pushed with all that was left at the spinning black circle.

Hands reached out, grappled, then grabbing at me. My hands, too weak and slippery, they went for my sleeves and collar.

A yank and a pull—I was out.

They all looked the same. They all do to us on the other side. A homeless-man pulled at me again and sat me down.

A moment later I was stripped. Life-giving flames radiated through cut-out holes from an old oil barrel.

I'd faced the waters again, looked at death. It'd found me again, and I'd broken through into a new life. The flames cured me. They sealed in a resurging strength. The shapes around the fire knew I wasn't one of them. My outer layers, stained, torn and tired, now hung out drying. They saw a different type of outcast in me.

I was laid bare in front of them.

My muscles flexed. With tattoos and scars mattifying as my limbs dried.

A power reawakened and they moved back wondering what they'd pulled from the water. They instinctively knew that I wasn't one of *those... out there*. The same demons that walked the streets past them each night. Another layer of rejected society. Those drug dealers that worked the alleyways perpetuating the poisons, fuelling the addicts; keeping them on the street.

My saviour had no chance of getting a break back to some normality. Circumstance had put him, and all of them, out in the cold. The ignorance of the city married with the ruthlessness of the pushers, thugs and gangs kept them there—pushing them deeper and deeper.

I felt a new purpose, to push back at it all: Mr. Big's drug-pushing hold over his domain. It felt like destiny that I should be pulled from here, one of his dumping grounds. Sure to die, saved by the bottom tier of his victims; the forgotten layers in his effect over the city.

Now, I was dead to those that so despised me.

I gave away everything from my wallet. The next morning I returned and gave them more.

I regrouped, drank coffee, smoked and bled. It ran from me carrying all the fear and love that had been holding me back. Cherry, and chances with her of my own normality had created a hesitance and humanity that I needed to forget to get the job done. My fears were born from knowing their hold over everything and what they were capable of. I needed to fuel off of this and rise up, or lower myself to what I knew I was capable off: checkmate them. Painted a darker shade of black inside.

I meant to face them head-on. A collision of their histories and mine. None of my weaknesses would reside anymore—I'd bled those out.

I had returned from the dead.

The girl I tried to save... and the boy. Both didn't stand a chance. I owed it to them. I should have been there to catch.

My thoughts returned to the girl in the hospital. And I was still thawing as I returned to St Lawrence.

18

This Is Music

THERE WERE LYRICAL forms and beauty in her hurt.

I saw inspiration in the depths of agony. The poetry in her angst. She held a perfect balance between pleasure and pain. Had an aesthetic surrounding her. It was both alluring and fear-inducing.

A trapped moth fluttered against the glass in front of her. Words left her in a stream of consciousness; becoming more ordered with each passing moment.

Eventually, the words stopped overlapping. Their beautiful canvasses of blues and reds lead me further into her world with a stone-cold staccato.

Up until that point I would get rid of my own demons by writing them out. With the girl, I'd become someone else's portal. I looked to purify her world. I shared the load. I took the daggers of pain, her thoughts and demons tormenting her.

She told me how they'd got involved with an underground club. They'd been introduced to it by their flatmates and friends in the block. Horrified at first, they'd later all come round to the notions of new and hidden pleasures to be found in pain. She told me of the first night they saw it up close. She and the boy's then seemingly conventional lovemaking, at that stage, had been interrupted—they had stopped mid-flow.

She described coldly in detail what happened.

The boy's face had come up for air, her legs had parted as she released the grip on his head. Both of their expressions had changed from intense and concentrated pleasure, to a puzzled worry.

This was the event that sparked a further chain of events leading her to be here now—an empty shell.

The boy was stolen from her by those pains they'd been introduced to.

'We thought we could smell burning bacon. That someone had left the pan on,' she said. 'The smoke alarm started and we both jumped up... I tripped over, treading on my panties around my ankles. He went first, opening the door, taking my hand. Sometimes I liked to let him think he was in control. Halfway down the corridor, he slowed and I took the lead back—I pulled him on. Like our lovemaking I suppose; no constant dominant one. We both had control—as it should be.'

She paused for breath. And stared as if re-seeing the events again...

'We waited before opening the kitchen door. Despite assuming the obvious, something in us knew there was more to it. The smoke alarm was still going but we didn't hear it anymore. There was just that smell. The smell of burning. Burning bacon... So we'd thought. It wasn't though.'

'What was it?' I asked, already assuming what was to come. 'Dave was a beautiful black man. We all loved him. So did our flatmate, Tracey. He sat on the worktop, half an arse cheek on the hob that had been left on. She was down on him and they were joined together in this new ugly type of ecstasy we hadn't seen before. His skin burning away. I wish we hadn't seen it. We should have stayed in his flat that night; not go to mine. We could have ignored the alarm and smell; put it down to another false alarm—broken toasters in the place were always setting them off.'

'The club: S.I.' I said, 'Sado… Intimacy?' 'Yes.'

We paused.

We were caught in a moment, created by the darkest of confessionals: they'd been introduced to the Devil. And, instead of walking away… they had embraced the darkness before them. A moral mistake leading to an inevitable conclusion. And with that, she was trapped in her existence forever… and he was dead.

'Does it still go on?'

She didn't answer at first. Her train of thought had finished for a moment, despite a pause for respite.

'They had a book, Towns of the Red Mist, I think… something like that. They changed the text to suit their wants… Their needs. You've read the original?' she asked.

'I might have dipped in and out of it.'

'Best you had, maybe. They used to quote it at meetings. I don't think it goes on now. Will's fall finished it for good.'

'Fall?'

'It was his fall from grace; humanity. He took the book, and the changes they made to it, to have real meaning. They edited it, chopped it about, added meaning where there wasn't any, and enhanced any that actually was there. They cited it—it became their guidance. Unlike the Bible guiding towards the light, it rooted us all firmly in the darkness. A darkness that exists in all of us but few rarely indulge. Not beyond fictional escapism: book or film. It changed how we looked at the world; steered both of us and all of them. Our lives lived, deaths… died.'

'His death,' I said.

'His most of all. It finished belief in it all. When we all saw where it was going. He'd just got there first. That book was written over so much, chopped and changed, it was hard to see where the original text lay and our polluted thoughts had taken over. None of us knew who was making the text changes one week to the next. The master copy was left in the basement of the flats on a wooden chair. It was there when we left and it was there when we returned each time with new edits, changes and directions scrawled in the sides. All over the top and between the lines. The last time we looked it had an account reworked and glorified for us.'

I listened hard as each of her words grew more and more heavy.

'It talked of a visitor to a remote jungle village. This place was untouched by the world's sensibility and rationales. We took this visitor to be us. The visitor watched on over a ceremony there where the village's old folks were slowly drawn between two horses. It was a slow death, but they didn't wince in pain. Instead they smiled as a euphoric rise took over them. Beneath each of them as they were ripped apart, were young couples fucking... Slowly, like the dying happening above them. The idea was that any conception would transfer the soul of the drawn out and torn apart into the new baby conceived. And so, a generation is transferred from one to another in the lovemaking below; a reincarnation.'

The air grew still in the room.

'When we opened the kitchen door that night... and saw them both, we were that visitor to the village. And like him, we could have walked away. But, like him, we stayed; leaving the outside world behind us. We watched, letting the momentum, the evil, take over us.'

'What happened to Will—why'd he go over like that?'

'He had worked himself up—pleasured himself until he was just right—then he jumped over and off that roof. He must have thought his soul would transfer to some other place or dimension. Maybe... he thought a little bit of himself would be implanted in a multitude of little fucks that were going on in the blocks at the time. The rugby was on. Most people didn't give a fuck. But everyone pretended to be staying in to watch it. We knew what we, and they, were really doing.'

'You... were right there... with him,' I hesitated. And I left.

I hoped that she'd expelled the last of it. I knew I was the only one to have heard her side: that they'd found some sort of evil happiness in slavery in a group sordid ideal.

I hoped she'd heal. Move on. Live.

An editor of that book on the chair in the basement had killed the boy. And I was sure it was a mutual enemy of mine. I saw signs everywhere. My therapist would call this confirmation bias.

To me, it was my fate.

I WENT BACK to the apartment and put on the tape, what was once Dire Straits' 'Brothers in Arms', now 'Black Bacon'. Another title that had been made obvious to me. I wanted to hear the thoughts of whoever was working the caretaker's position on the day the girl and boy's lives were taken over... by the S.I. movement.

Turned out it was very short... and sweet:

'Idiots... set the alarm off again! Went on forever. They were all stood outside getting wet for the firemen so I let myself in. They normally set it off with their toasters. This time; bacon stuck to the hob. Beautiful blackened... salty bacon. The fire brigade charged past me on the stairs on the way up. I was still picking the scraps of it from my teeth on the way down. I went straight into The Woolpack. I had a pint and told Jimmy about the dumb fucks.'

(Licking lips noise)

'… *Tasty bacon though.*'

(Swallows, gulps.)

'… *Tasty. Black. Bacon.*'

19

(Hankster) The Gangster

FORMATIVE YEARS:

At first, Brandon wasn't the top dog at school. He cracked a few heads; nothing special. One lad didn't speak without drooling again—no big deal. He had to work at his craft; his excellence and position took time to take hold over him, the others and his surroundings.

Initially, the already established bully-boys targeted him for his quiet demeanour. Naively they saw him as easy prey; a shy boy. The message soon spread that he was more of a challenge. Then more lined up, wanting to prove themselves. They queued up for it, lemmings to the fall—idiots. And a rights-of-passage for him, as he honed his skills.

Once, and only once, a teacher had him up in front of the class. In hindsight maybe it was a turning point for Brandon, the school too. It certainly was for the teacher's ability to walk. Up on top of his desk at the front, the idiot gave him ten good ones with a size thirteen Dunlop Green Flash. It wasn't the first time he'd used it either. The soles were split from his repeated action across generations of kids' legs and arses.

Actually, it wasn't his fault, not that time. It was the boy sitting next to him that squirted the acid down the back of the girl's coat in front. It didn't matter to Brandon, he took the hits for it.

Later, he used it to manipulate the boy who had done it; made him his runner for a bit. Looking back, he'd gotten off lightly. That same lad followed him all the way to Manchester too, became a doer, driver, and odd jobber. It's funny how much fear and loyalty can accomplish, that and a manipulated sense of guilt.

The lad died on a collection a few years back. He'd pleaded to get out and retire in the weeks leading up to it. Brandon had paid another lad to take him out. Stuck with an ice pick to the eye. *Want to retire do you? Here you are*, he'd thought. Besides… he knew too much. He'd too much baggage from those early years on Brandon.

John-fucking-Black knew too much too.

He didn't bother with the lad's funeral back then. Didn't matter if they'd been together since those old school days. Brandon had somewhere else to be. If he knew the boy's sister, he would've probably been there.

He enjoyed taking the hits. And the girls looking at him whilst the teacher dished out his punishment—his best. He smiled at them. His grins were full of intent as each hardening stroke to his arse cheeks came down. They saw it in his eyes… he was imagining the spanking he was giving *them* in his dirty mind.

It only got deeper and dirtier from then on. He grew to act on his thoughts. The realities often outshone the fantasies.

Later that night he paid the teacher, Mr 'soon-to-have-a-permanent-limp' Pearce, a little visit at his home. He was still holding that condescending look in his eyes, and a copy of some shitty broadsheet rag, as he opened the door. He must have expected a canvasser or a Jehovah's Witness. The crowbar soon wiped that stupid fucking look off his face. The paper crumpled in his grip then fell to the floor. His kneecap followed.

He couldn't remember the words he whispered in the teacher's ear as he cried for mercy. Probably a threat to him and his closest. To keep a lid on it.

There was no further dressing down in class for Brandon. And he didn't feel the need to attend more either. No one had any more to say on the matter.

By the end of the last term, he led over them all, teachers too, with a primal fear. There was a community brewing outside the school too. It just needed showing the way.

One time he was going for a smoke with Martin down by the river—it beat going to any class. Some lanky fuck and little cunt had him against a wall. They must have thought they'd challenge the order of things. He stared down the short-arse, who fancied himself to be Joe Pesci in Goodfellas. He soon backed off; seeing Brandon's blackening eyes. Then, he kicked through the knee of the lanky tall one; made him cry like a baby—they thought it was all over for them.

But it wasn't quite. Not for Brandon.

He wanted them to remember; for people to see the scars. And to know he wasn't to be fucked with.

He used what was to hand: a rusty tin lid and a fag that had fallen from Martin's mouth, as his mouth had dropped open with the sheer violence of it all.

Thing is Brandon's mum and dad had shown him how to give and take it all his life. It was like business as usual at home. So, it was just child's play at school. As the appetite for dishing it out grew and was set, so was his path to glory.

AFTER HITTING THE streets of Manchester and Salford it wasn't long before those that would have previously challenged him, lined up to be with him. A path of least resistance. He burned a few pairs of feet with a blowtorch. And he ironed some to the bone on ironing boards for a few days. It didn't take much. They got the message.

Word got around...

He still drilled a few knee caps, took the golf clubs to the balls of a few here and there—that was just for fun now though. A reinforcement of the message.

And with that, word soon spread further afield. He was... and is... the Mr Big of these cities.

The heat came down on them, because of Black, but rumour had it among the boys there was another snitch on the doors; a rat. And he grabbed the newest lad. It helped his motives knowing he was one of Black's friends—if he had such things; cold-hearted fuck.

He did everything to that boy he wanted to do to Black. He hung him up in his favourite abandoned factory in the Northern Quarter. Few had been there and come out alive, other than him and a trusted few. Those who were invited along were there to carry out the torture when he ran tired, or just wanted to watch.

The boy he grabbed had only worked the doors a few days. Black and he had shared a round from the bar. And smiled in agreement on an occasion and that was enough to seal his fate. All suspicions and paranoias were taken out on and absorbed by his body.

The heavies strung him up by the wrists and naked, leaving him like that for four days... until the strength to fight, survive or give in had gone. Then, Mr. Big entertained himself.

When he ran out of holes to put the soldering iron, he made new ones with mindless cutting. Growing bored of that he stabbed him to the chest. He used his fingers between the hilt of the blade so it just went far enough in...but didn't kill. The next hours; best part of a day, were spent fingering and toying with that hole. And whispering in the boy's ear, all as if he was to blame for the downfall of his state and kingdom.

As if he was John Black himself.

He pushed against his struggling heart as it tried to beat out and muttered venomous spit covered angst in his ear.

The boy was in purest hell.

20

Substance

MR BIG WAS a criminal's criminal… Chopper's Chopper and more Bronson than Bronson. He was known to me, the police and his own puppets as well as the jury I put him up in front of. And that was it. Other than that he was a feared echo throughout the City's underbelly. Every city has one, labelled up by the press as the City's alpha male to rule its underworld. If you think you've heard of this one. You haven't.

There are tiers and layers to society, strata beneath us all that the public aren't made aware of. Like in politics, those that truly pull the strings—behind closed doors, from yachts, islands, and out of sight.

There's one in Manchester, Liverpool and Newcastle—all just labels. A brand to excite the masses, to convince them there's a common enemy on the streets. An achievable foe for the authorities.

This Mr Big was more than a label. He was my Nemesis.

He was the Puppet Master and orchestrator of most of my pain since leaving. All names have been changed to protect the guilty as they say—I've given mine no *real* name at all. When I was involved with it all, working for them, you could tell the origins of messages, and that they'd come from him. The expressions that gripped the runners' faces, and the content carried with it confirmed it.

I'd met him a few times. I'd expected him to have a services background too. If he had, he'd bulked out a bit for sure; done his time in Abra-kebab-ra as well as Strangeways. He'd evolved into a dangerous mix of power and weight with it. Although, he rarely needed or got the opportunity to throw it about any more.

Back then he'd pay mugs like me to do that, keeping his hands clean. Sometimes he'd indulge, like taking a golf club or nail bar to someone's shins. He'd pull a tooth or three, or stick a dart in someone's eye or testicle as they were held down writhing in pain. He'd wear petrol station disposable gloves for that type of work. And he'd always get a heavy to eat them afterwards, like the car tape. It became one of his tropes.

His conscience was black. As black as mine... then some.

His reach was so far, wide and dirty—woven into every little and large bit of supply and demand across the City. I was sure he was connected to the S.I. thing; he'd be a sponsor, donor, ring leader, or conductor. What I couldn't see was how he was to make anything from it; money, reputation, or anything of worth.

Maybe, doing evil was enough for him.

The devil isn't a finite person or a thing. Like Mr. Big, it's a title, assigned when needed, so we might better digest the delivery of evil. A noxious substance. The devil is the coat on the meat. The blood and bones of our evil, as it walks our streets. When the coat opens up you either look away or get drawn into it. And so it masses out, growing with each person it consumes. And then they contribute, getting a taste for it.

A taste for the black meat.

Entering a city you can sense whether it has an imbalance in it. If there are more people under the coat, in its embrace than outside of it looking the other way—walking a different line. For now, this was Manchester.

I meant to cut the head from the beast; return balance to the City.

I WANTED TO finish my drink in O'Shea's Irish bar and go back to look in the basement of the block of flats. I was apprehensive, but knew there would be a book there. I was hoping to soak up the atmosphere and get a feeling for all that had happened up until the boy's jump (push or fall). The event that released a grip on the block's residents by the S.I. club.

I wasn't aiming directly at him yet.

Aiming low, I disintegrated what was below and holding the target up. The target would surely drop, drop and drop some more to me; to be within my sights. By then it would be up to me, pull the trigger or let it fall out. And wait for what was next to come down. Such is the life of the pessimistic optimist.

I hadn't realised the next pint was there and that I hadn't moved on. People to the left and right of me were knocking back oysters with their Guinness—not for me. I'd sooner try a strip of blackened bacon than knocking back that sea filth. All just salted squid's ass, used rubbers and gull's phlegm.

A poster for a club night called Wonder Lust caught my eye as I left. With it, I thought how close we were to crossing the line all the time… It's just a curiosity away. Or, as is the case of the many uber-rich growing bored of the obvious, there's that level to cross into. Society's boundaries of taste and moral constraints were just other items on the menu. To some, just another foul-tasting oyster to be knocked back before moving onto burnt flesh and the pleasure and pain game.

For me, the Marquis De Sade shit was just a hidden track on the CD of life that wasn't needed. But… if you lose focus, fall asleep in the complacency of life, you're then confronted by it and caught out.

People never failed in their ability to disappoint, disgust and surprise me. Sometimes though, innocents, like the boy got stuck in a mechanism. The cogs of the City, its moments, and a time and place would grind them to dust in a horror show.

On my way back I stopped into the Black Horse. I had beef with the last caretaker for running out on me last time.

He was there, full of drink and fixed to his usual spot. He mumbled something self-pitying, drunken and semi- meaningful about whiskey and being shot.

We've all been shot.

I broke his nose and left.

21

Some Velvet Morning

CHERRY KNEW IT was a mistake to go to him.

Everyone at the station kept saying he was made for that role. They joked: 'Is he on witness protection from the Manchester mob or them from him?'

It was true, he'd done service, was hardened, and by his time in the underworld... Damn it, he was still stuck there; in both places. His morality and loyalty had proved a weakness to them, they took advantage. Then it blew up, for everyone involved...

A girl had died and his identity was wiped—if it was ever his true name. Manchester had folded in on him. Once his mother, now an iron maiden closing slowly into his chest.

Cherry had seen another side to him. Behind Black's eyes there was the man that wanted to move on. Wanted a life. She hoped... in part, it was with her. There was more past the scars, there *he* was: the writer.

She went to The Hatchett to see his so-called agent.

She told M. Pampelmousse she was on her way to Manchester—to see him. The Landlady looked as close to shocked as an ex-burlesque stripper could. Then she reached under the bar and slid an old revolver over. When Cherry refused to take it she simply poured two very large scotches, and they sat in silence. Then it was time for Cherry to go catch a train.

She'd wished she'd taken the gun.

As she opened the door to the caretaker's flat, it wasn't John there. It was *him*. She'd taken the journey hoping to pull John from hell.

As Mr Big grinned, the shadows of his crew appeared behind her. She realised all she'd done is throw herself right in there—into her very own hell.

He simply grinned some more and raised an index finger. In his other hand was John's first book. He stared at her, unblinking, and he wagged his finger... slowly; like a parent to a toddler.

A postie entered the lobby behind them, and without looking put parcels and a clipboard down on the writing shelf. Still, without looking he foolishly barked for a signature. A big mistake. He should have run. They grabbed him, took him off to another room. Unlike her, he was disposable. He hadn't even looked up to identify them, but they wouldn't take the chance. Besides, it was a bit of fun. Like slicing a traffic warden. Anything in uniform was game.

She wasn't going to give them anything on John. If they didn't have it already. This meant she was in for pain, and worse. Having her and letting Black know as much was enough. And everything they were going to do to her, was extra and for their own entertainment. Something to pass the time, whilst getting John prepared to sniff the bait.

She reached for her radio in her pocket.

'Now now, naughty, naughty... Very fucking naughty,' he said. 'You don't want me going back inside that quickly do you? We're gonna have us some fun first. Besides you'd miss me.'

'When he catches back up with you, you won't be going back in.'

'Really?'

'You'll be dead,' she trembled. He laughed.

They pulled the blinds down on the reception room. Dust and dead flies flew out into the room. The hatch was closed and the door locked softly.

Darkness closed in around her.

A Zippo flicked on under his chin. There was a madness in his grin and eyes, as he drooled in anticipation and relished her torment. He wiped his mouth and touched her lips with the drool.

'Boo,' he whispered, an inch from her face. And he flicked the flame off again.

They all laughed. Shoved her. Stroked at her hair.

She cried out with fear. But only on the inside—she was giving them nothing.

22

Archives of Pain

THE BASEMENT DOOR was a black monolith.

I breathed out and blackness breathed me in. A light flickered barely illuminating the chair in the centre of the dingy room—and there was the book. Walking slowly, I felt the pain, lust, and depravity. With the book at its core. I neared, slowly and picked it up. Before I turned it over, I knew it was going to be mine:

Untethered.

It was part of the game being played around me... It was planted, it was a sign. They were showing me they knew I was going to be there.

'Why not publish a diary, with all your thoughts and weaknesses? Then, put it into your enemies' hands?' I thought out loud to the shadows, 'Because... you want to die,' I answered back. 'Them too,' I finished.

Untethered was never meant to be published, but the ex-burlesque stripper back in Bristol had convinced me. She told me the filth and scum in that dirty old town would love it— some did. Some not so much.

A lot of its story is what could have been if I'd answered an old question from my childhood with my gut, rather than my conscience. It was a path almost taken or a parallel existence. The rest is a reality of sorts and what sounds unbelievable to some is likely truth to others. The fact is I was lost and found in there; in writing it. The process was killing me, whilst revealing the real me at the same time.

That question, that came from the past was: 'What do you want to be when you grow up? I told them I wanted to be in the army: the SAS.

My grandmother said, 'you'll have to kill people, a lot of people, would you really like to do that?'

I'd said, 'No, but...they'd be bad people. Right?'

They tried to get me to kill. I didn't. I'd get there in the end.

I LEFT THE basement and went straight to the girl again. 'How long has my book been there?'

There was little to get from her before she started to rip at her eyes, touching herself again. According to her, the book was always the Towns of the Red Mist, or similar by a U.S. Beat poet. It was never the Möbius strip of a confessional by me.

With the girl of little use I went back to the Black Horse. I'd have to play softer than last time if I was to get anything from the ex-caretaker.

I was still ready to break bones too.

When I arrived he'd changed, complete with a cold stare. Despite the empties in front of him he looked sober, stronger somehow, more confident—too fucking confident.

Of course he was in on it. The tough nutter had played me; pretending to be washed up, a weakened waster with no part in it all. Now I saw him.

He'd taken the broken nose.

Pain meant nothing—there was a bigger game, more pains elsewhere if he didn't play his part.

'Take a seat,' he said pushing a stool out. 'Drink!' And one came. 'You know, there's those that 'ave missed you Black. Then there's those... hmm. Shall we say: not so much. Which do you think there's more of?'

'Depends which barmaid you ask I guess.'

'Cut the shit.'

I paused. They had me. I needed to hear him out.

He went on, 'Remember Big Tony on the estate? The Barber? Only knew one cut: number three buzz cut all over. One of your door-pals mentioned your name, thinking he'd get an even cheaper cut... Well, he did alright. Tony cut his neck with a straight razor to the spine just at the mention of your fucking name. He'd only been out a week—one of the boys you'd helped get a lighter sentence for information.'

'Chris,' I muttered.

'They just left him there to bleed out. The rest stepped over him to get their cuts before the end of the day... and didn't give a fuck. There was hair and black pudding all over the place by the end of the day.'

I feigned ignoring the provocation, and returned: 'What was with the sob story earlier? You seeing if I'd follow suit... open up... join in the drinking, cry and pour it out. All my scars, bullets, stories and pains too. Didn't go as planned, did it? Only got your nose broken.'

'To find what made you tick... Or at least to distract you long enough so things could be moved around without you interfering,' he stated, stared then downed a double. 'More,' he pointed and it came. 'You see, you won't take the obvious beating and attempts at your life. And, this game isn't as simple as cat versus rat. There are about a hundred thousand cats and only one rat... And someone wants you to suffer. Guess who?'

'Yeah... well he's got his coming too.'

'How long d' you think you're gonna last?'

'About this long,' I said through gritted teeth and had him by the windpipe. As I squeezed he didn't look any different. Eyes bold, reddened over a little but he made no attempt at a concession: I knew he was a patsy. A distraction.

'Say your piece fucker,' I spat at him, 'where am I meant to be? Or, are the doors gonna lock here and everyone's gonna turn on me? Because if they do, one thing's for sure—you're going first!'

'Patience... patience John,' he rasped and rubbed his throat. 'Ever been fishing in France John?'

'No,' my impatience was growing too much. I shook and he could see it.

'Brutal, the French. Particularly with food. Funny, and here we are in the Black Horse. The fuckin' horse eaters really are evil in catching their damn dirty food.'

'Get to it, before I start breaking the rest of you,' I said, wondering if I had enough space to swing the glass ashtray at his knee cap then his shin.

'Shark fishing... in France,' he continued. 'You see the brutal Frenchies, to catch a meal of shark fin soup, have a little cruelty they deploy. Want to know what it is? I'll tell you anyway... It's banned. Doesn't stop them. Sick fuckers. Perhaps they're married to it and it's in their blood—the brutality of it all. They've a rather cruel...' he paused to think of a word to use, 'uncivil, yes uncivil way to catch sharks: barbaric you could say.'

'Cut the shit,' I said as my hands tightened on the edge of the bar stool.

'The principle is universal—simple. Transferable you might even say—useful in our situation here even: distress one thing to bring another out into the open and then catch it too. You know what they do John? They thread a fishing hook through the back tendons of a live cat or dog and drag it behind a boat. The blood and distress attract sharks from miles around. Just like you Johnny-boy. Just. Like. You.'

I gasped; paused. I held the moment.

'That book of yours gives it all away John. Where you were hiding—the witness protection. How and who you hate... And, who you love. All leverage John. Bait on the line. A cut-up pussy dangling on a fucking line... For the sharks.'

The air seemed to thicken as I struggled to take a breath. 'How far will the *Cherry* drop John... Before getting so bruised no one will want to touch it? Your fuckin' *Cherry*...' I breathed out, held it there.

'The boy's drop... Who gives a fuck. We've saved the true horror show, just for you!'

I skipped the knees and shins. And, went straight for the head. I ran out and didn't look back. The door shut behind me before he'd hit the floor. The ashtray was embedded in his skull and his crushed left eye hung down a cheek. Vitreous and blood mixed with an afternoon's fag ash.

23

The Bends

I RAN OUT against a hard rain and was sick into it. The force of the wind and rain changed direction; pushing me into a bush. Laughter came from a nearby poverty filled McDonald's. The fat hung from their hands as the blood dripped from mine.

With a gasp and a push, I was up and going on again.

Why did she come here?... Because of me. I did this to her.

On the block of flats' rooftop, he had her over the edge. A belt was around her neck and he had her dangling, one foot barely on the ledge as she was hanging out. Her own weight was strangling her. Blood dripped down the back of her jeans. And a mix of this and worse was over her ankles.

'Never liked them much. WPCs. One that's into you even less. This way, it's a bonus. I get you and this. The FILTHY... PIG. BITCH.' and he spat over her hair.

'Hello,' I said, bent double and was sick again.

He flicked the safety off on the Glock he gripped in his other hand, and opened with his speech: 'Remember that boy you worked our doors with at the end John... you had him go to the bar for you... a friend, was he? Anyway... unlucky bastard was just stood too close to your world wasn't he. Playing at being a police rat too. Right little understudy wasn't he?'

I took a deep breath.

'He wasn't meant for this,' he continued, looking around as if surveying his domain from the vantage point of the rooftop. 'He was a part-time student or something. Or was that why you took him under your wing. To dissuade him from working full time with us. Well... ner' mind. I cut him up real good, John— burnt the fuck outa him, pretending he was you. Another one of your victims in the end John. We resuscitated him two or three times; each time told him we wouldn't again. We gave up in the end, got bored. It just wasn't the same. Just wasn't you. I had to leave... We went to force a blow-job from that barmaid that served you both. You did that to them, John. Both, my gift to you. And this... this bitch.'

I spat, glaring.

'Ha, beautiful isn't it... The way it's all come together like this,' he said.

I looked up through the hell he'd made. And my bloodshot eyes blackened over.

The Viking readied himself to charge.

'She's turning blue John... Whatever you're gonna do...do it!' and with each word, he let his grip on the belt slip so she went a fraction more out...further over the edge.

I became more aware of the gun he held in his left hand, limiting my options. It was bandaged and dripping blood; she must have fought back—she was like that.

Really, there was only one way this was going.

'This is giving me a hard-on John... finish this,' he spat and took aim, 'God this city hates you, John. It's time. Put us all out of your misery.'

'What happens... when an unstoppable force...meets an immovable object Brandon?' I asked.

He winced at the sound of his *real* name.

Maybe he hadn't heard it spoken out loud since school. And it conjured up buried memories of his own.

Doubt and fear appeared behind his eyes. I forced myself up and at him.

24

Live Forever

WE CAME OUT to a crowd made up of the city's underworld. Past and present, Cheetham Hill's, Moss Side's, China Town's, and other rival gangs' bosses all stood there. Those working their way through the ranks were at the back.

They'd wanted to watch the fall. Someone had put a shout out that there was something, and someone, going down. They wanted to see the outcome, him or me, for themselves. I wished I'd taken his gun before he went over. I'd used his own weight against him and pulled her back from the edge. There was nothing to spare in the exchange. She had already turned into a mix of blue and red, and there had been no time to waste.

He'd got a round or three off. One missed, the others became new additions to my collection of scars. Who knows how: her weight pulling at him, the rain, being caught up in the moment itself. All must have unsteadied his aim. The injured hand she'd given him will have played a part too. Deep inside part of me thought he just wasn't as set on killing me as all that though.

And, at that moment, when he saw them turn up, and all waiting downstairs… That then he decided to make some grand final exit.

Blood, sweat and tears shone on our skins as I could barely hold her up. The last of my strength was helped by something else, making it possible. We staggered forward hesitantly and wearily into the lion's den and the eye of the crowd.

We awaited their action. Although we felt as though judgment had already been passed on us; our fates sealed.

Unmarked squad cars appeared in the background and meant nothing. The city's underworld carried enough sway and fire-power to turn any tide that might go against them.

The base of the flats formed the start of the drama, horror and pains for the boy and his mother. Now it was to be our own journey's end.

In the background, my Viking hacked away at the bloody mass that was once the body of my enemy. Sprays of crimson splashed up and over the backs of men who stood by. We stared on, stood still, and faced-off the horseshoe-shaped rabble, mainly made up of hard-faced men. But for a few. One or two female bosses, a DJ I recognised from jabbing me in the leg, and children, their future sealed, tainted; now runners and mules for the gangs.

An eerie stillness held us all between the two towers which were blocking the wind. The rain continued, it streamed down, bouncing between the blocks and hit us hard.

I knew the face that walked forward: one of his many damaged and scarred surrogate sons—like me. He'd given rise to a few. Brandon didn't let them go easily, me neither. It was a job for life and death.

He held out a shaking hand. It grasped a bloodied rag.

The others looked down.

This was a ceremony.

My gut told me what was in the rag and Cherry shook her head for me not to accept it.

I took it, we turned, then walked.

A few crooked cops were on the sidelines and stepped up their duties to help carry Cherry as we passed by. Guilt drove them or maybe they saw me as their new boss—whichever side

I ended up on.

More blue lights came and the crowd stared.

I dropped the gold tooth and finger with a familiar signet ring down the nearest drain. I still bear the scar on my right eyebrow from a previous encounter with that ring.

The 'T' on the knuckle of his 'Love and Hate' tattoos was the last I saw of my inherited trophies.

My gesture meant nothing. They waited for my next move. For now, having removed the head of the beast—I had become *Mr Big*.

IN TIME, I sent the tapes, with one of my own, to the boy's mother. I added a note to say, if she wanted to sleep at all—to avoid the horror; let it be, leave them alone. And when she couldn't, to listen to mine first. Parts of it M. Pampelmousse took for this book, changing enough to protect the guilty.

EVENTUALLY, THE RAIN would stop... then it would start again. Someone else would die. And I would be on another train, even further North. I was going home.

25

Transference

SHE WASN'T SCARED. It was in her eyes.

I must have lost it, Brandon thought.

Back in the day, she'd have lost her shit at the mere mention of his name. Now, he was in front of her, doing his best evil-face... Zippo under his chin, complete darkness flowing out of him. And there was nothing.

I've definitely, maybe... fuckin' lost it.

It's a sign.

And, with Black being back, the city vibrated with his energy. It was like the Antichrist had arrived. He'd made it clear: he wouldn't die... or change sides. What happened with the canal... the car as well. What the fuck? He just wouldn't...roll-over.

That's it. He is...the fucking Antichrist.

The boys were starting to go to work on her, trying to spook her up. They were telling her what they were gonna do. Real nasty like.

He sat, watched, puzzled... This didn't fit.

They hadn't done anything yet but she hadn't cracked. It was usually the anticipation and fear that got to people. The actual act was a conclusion and people had normally given up by then, left as gibbering wrecks.

They got to spitting, pulling a nail out and whispering in her ears. She was still rock solid; no fear. Damn it, she was a hard one. She was real-strong. He really fucking admired that. And wished he'd had some like her on his crew.

He reached over to the arm of the sofa, picked up the copy of John's book, and started to flick through it. Pure shit, the lot of it... Confused and self-confessing shite.

It angered him. At first...

Then... came a mention of the stint in Ireland.

He froze and focussed his eyes. They started to speed over the pages, absorbing each and every detail. Then, Brandon's breath stilled as his eyes tightened in on the individual letters: I.R.A.

He read that John refused to fire on them. It was in a fire-fight outside a church... He got burnt and shot up pretty bad too doing it—and that's why they let him go. Not because he was hurt. Because he wouldn't fire back. They had them outnumbered, and they were in his sights. Stubborn... hard bastard.

So... that's how he ended up in Manchester and working the clubs. Brandon's club.

It was destiny.

Brandon knew it now.

HIS BROTHER HAD been over in Ireland; fought with the other side. He used to tell this crazy story of a fire-fight... outside a church. This mad bastard on the other side got all shot and burnt up, by not fighting back. He swore, it wasn't because he was scared. He said, he could see his brothers in those crazy eyes facing back at him. He could even see Brandon deep in them, over that distance, down the barrel of his rifle. And there was something else... His brother would joke, as he described the flames getting higher and higher around this guy.

He saw this damn image, spectre, ghost or demon in the

flames: it was a Viking. Right there, plain as sight, staring right back at him from the flames.

They had her jeans down, bent her over and were about to move things on. It was base level torture shit—and he was bored. His mind was opening. He now saw another reality in all of this. The sides weren't as they'd seemed. The gods of war had stacked the cards against them. Black wasn't meant to lose. The bullets, the flames didn't kill him over there. They couldn't over here either. He was meant for higher things.

He wasn't made to fire back at them, his kin. And so, he burned for them.

'Stop!' he cut in, 'NOW!' and he went over, moved them aside. He flicked out a knife as they panted eagerly in anticipation. He hated them for that. Normally, this would be his moment to revel. And they always spoiled it, like lap dogs over a prime cut of steak.

Something had ruptured in his brain. A clot or burst vessel and it pained him: a morality had crept in, taking hold. Roots of something out of his normal nature. Now, both of them were just heathen dogs to him.

He sliced deep into his hand, savoured the pain then let it drip. He wiped the blood across her jeans, and arse cheeks, then aimed it to run down her crack. He let some go down and over her ankles, squeezing hard. He wanted John to think the worst when they next met.

Then, and only then, would he fulfil the new role: his destiny. The lads looked confused as he told them what they had to do: 'Put the call out, go get them... ALL of them!' was the message, 'bring the gangs and their leaders.' Cherry looked up at him, unflinching, stone-cold. *So damn strong.*

He popped the little blue pill and waited for the blood to start pumping. His hand slid into his pocket. He slowly stuck the blade of the knife into his leg as the Viagra started to take effect. He felt the arousal heightened as more blood started to trickle from the cut to his thigh. He was too late to this club... Maybe there was something in this whole S.I. shit after all. It was practically made for him.

By not firing back; saving Brandon's brother in Ireland, as far as he was concerned John's fate was sealed—what better reward for the damn Antichrist. John could take the mantle.

He was born for this.

He heard them start to pull up outside. The pill had done its work. His itching appendage pushed hard, gnawing at the zip from the inside to be set free. Like a caged hungry beast.

It had been a long day.

John better take the bait... He will have got the message by now from my boy, Mark, in the Black Horse.

Slowly he took off his belt, put it around her neck and tightened the buckle. As he walked her to the lift, he felt his grip over the city relax. It was all coming together. And he had somewhere to be: up top.

Calm spread throughout him. Serene. How he imagined a Zen master might feel at the top of a sacred mountain. The lift doors opened and he looked at her. Deep into her. With his eyes, he willed her to understand, to know what was happening.

He touched the ring on his finger and rubbed at the 'Love' and 'Hate' tattoos. He took the ring off, held it out, then returned it to his finger. She squinted, then opened wide as her icy statue-like expression cracked. The realisation had dropped. She seemed to read his mind, and with it her and John's dreams were destroyed...

Now, she looks scared.

IT WAS OBVIOUS to her, now, why she'd been left, almost untouched by their standards. But for the blood he dripped over the back of her. Brandon wanted John to think the very worst. If John was to carry out this insane master plan.

It was time. In Brandon's eyes she could see death, but not her or John's.

She didn't want the lift to move. The doors shut and the lights flickered off, on... then off again. They moved up in total darkness. She wanted it to get stuck, forever. Time to be frozen. But, as the stained lit up numbers changed, she knew the time had come. And, having summoned them all to bear witness, he meant to retire and transfer his Kingdom over to John Black.

The lift doors shuddered open.

She refused to open her eyes and make it real. Hiding from the darkness behind tightly closed eyes. A tear escaped, and for a moment was suspended in mid-air.

She saw that last kiss they should have had, on the train platform. Everyone deserves a last kiss.

Author's Note

In this case, as with the previous, I was mainly drunk, asleep and all the new altered states between the two I'd discovered on my way. This much I remember, the rest is from a notebook the suggested release by my therapist whilst I was on my previous vocation: under witness protection. I sent these notes to E.L. Noire (a.k.a Mademoiselle Pampelmousse), as always. She's a true force of nature. And, an ex-burlesque dancer. She's also a literary agent to the dark and dirty of humanity.

Be warned in all of this: what you think is true is probably made up. And vice versa.

An example:

Once, me and my equivalent of The Duke's 'Dr. Gonzo' were staggering back home the wrong way from a pub in Salford—it had been a long night and was already into the next morning.

Lights flashed overhead and a helicopter appeared, hitting the building's roof beside us. The heavens opened and we saw images of buildings reminiscent of Times Square in New York. We ran for cover past an out of context yellow cab, and straight into the nearest pub. It was stone dead in there—almost a ghost town bar. It was like a nuclear alarm bell had gone off and emptied the place. At no point did we question why it was open at all, way past closing time. Even the pub lock-in we'd been at had long since locked up. As we looked around, it was all way too familiar.

We ran back out into the rain and fell over on the cobbles outside, just as an American dressed copper appeared. He chased us whilst taking out an old revolver. Taking a breath we looked back across the road, to see he'd stopped his chase and was visibly laughing at us. Then, he waved us off with his hat and closed the giant gates across the street we'd just been on.

As it had happened, we had been wandering drunk and lost street to street, and unknowingly wandered into a very dilapidated, run down and soon to shut (for good), Granada Studios Tour. The eerie and disturbingly familiar pub had been The Rovers Return from Coronation Street.

Later, as we joked about our drunken idiocy, and still hoped our drunken beer compasses would point us home, a female football or hockey team threw their entire coach load of kits at us as they drove past. We were buried in the sweaty kit, and the puddle it had driven through. We were drenched in mud on top of the rain.

We woke later that morning with predictably banging heads, still fully dressed and one of us was less a shoe. I reached down to my legs, both covered in semi-dried on concrete up to the knees. My shoes were caked in it, and the whereabouts of my side kick's missing shoe had been made obvious: it had become a permanent fixture of the foundations to the adjacent housing estate being built alongside our block of flats.

I had ticket stubs and a club stamp for places I had no recollection of being at. As I looked at the TV that had been left on in front of me, there was a midget on a trampoline telling me the weather for the day—rain was coming… lots of it. But then, on top of the old set, worryingly, there was a black box flashing at me. At closer inspection, it was a car alarm that had been placed there. Cables hung from it like tendrils of an organ ripped out of a living body. It sat there flashing, centre stage for us and all our flatmates to see—like a trophy. A throbbing finger on my hand triggered a memory of ramming a Fiat 126 with a gas canister. The car had won; my finger lost—as was any reason for attacking it.

It's just that kind of random madness that can, and does, often happen. You can't make it up, because if you did people wouldn't believe you.

Such are the stories we tell each other. However, not all is as it seems. After all, life's reality is made fiction by memory. Especially, if you wait more than twenty years to write it down.

About the Author

John's writing has appeared online and in print for the likes of Red Dog Press, Bristol Noir, Close to the Bone, Storgy Magazine, Litro Magazine, Punk Noir Magazine, Necro Magazine and Deadman's Tome.

He grew up on the coast in rural Northumberland, a region steeped with a history of battles, Vikings, wars and struggles.

These tales and myths fascinated him as a child, and then as an adult. In the mid to late nineties he studied in Salford enjoying the bands, music, clubs and general urban industrialness of Greater Manchester, including the club scene and the infamous Hacienda. He was also there when the IRA bomb went off in 1996.

He's the founder and editor of the Bristol Noir e-zine which specialises in dirty realism, noir and dark fiction.

John lives in Bristol with his wife and daughters, where he has been since the late nineties. He is a professional designer, artist and writer as well as a proud husband, father, brother and son.

UNTETHERED, the first Black Viking thriller, is out now.

Lightning Source UK Ltd.
Milton Keynes UK
UKHW011921240221
379302UK00002B/84